INNER JOURNEY

Judy Lorraine Brown

DEDICATION

I dedicate this to all who have suffered, who have made the inner journey and chosen good over bad, right over wrong, and love over hate.

TABLE OF CONTENTS

CHAPTERS

	Preface	Pg 6
I	Jamie	Pg 9
II	The Move	Pg 20
III	Ronnie	Pg 54
IV	The Confrontation	Pg 64
V	Taking Charge	Pg 72
VI	First Touch	Pg 82
VII	Victoria	Pg 89
VIII	Summer Trip	Pg 96
IX	Shocking Truth	Pg 103
X	Alex	Pg 108
XI	The Return	Pg 119
XII	The Encounter	Pg 132
XIII	The Murder	Pg 145
XIV	Depression	Pg 150

XV	Mongo	Pg 159
XVI	The Admission	Pg 169
XVII	Erma and Mary	Pg 182
XVIII	The Runaway	Pg 189
XIX	The Escape	Pg 198
XX	The Attack	Pg 208
XXI	The Disposal	Pg 216
XXII	The Collapse	Pg 226
XXIII	The Separation	Pg 228
XXIV	Critical	Pg 235
XXV	The Dream	Pg 245
XXVI	Bitterness	Pg 256
XXVII	Rage	Pg 262
XXVIII	Agape	Pg 267
XXIX	Madness	Pg 271
XXX	The Plan	Pg 277
XXXI	The Ride	Pg 280
XXXII	The Response	Pg 285

XXXIII	Interrogation	Pg 295
XXXIV	Vietnam	Pg 303
XXXV	Help	Pg 306
XXXVI	Kidnap	Pg 315
XXXVII	Torture	Pg 320
XXXVIII	The Search	Pg 325
XXXIX	Hostage	Pg 329
XL	The Phone Call	Pg 332
XLI	Questions	Pg 337
XLII	The Fight	Pg 341
XLIII	The Answer	Pg 347
XLIV	The Letter	Pg 352
XLV	The End	Pg 355

ACKNOWLEDGMENTS

I acknowledge Evelyn Turner Maxey, my mother who gave me great strength, and fortitude. I acknowledge Father Victor Bieberle, who gave me a chance to acquire wisdom and showed me courage. I acknowledge Dwight Linton who has shown me true friendship and perseverance. I acknowledge my son Brian Lee Hauge who has always been my inspiration.

Preface

The hot water beating down upon her bruised torn skin stung, and burned, but the pain was good. It reminded her she was still alive. "God, if only I didn't have to leave this shower." "Never go back into the world again." "Just quietly die here where it is warm and clean; only the sound of running water."

The words seem to just bang around in her head like she was not in control of where they came from. This momentary escape from reality never lasted as long as she would have wished it to. She began to feel the water cool slightly in temperature, which was a subtle sign to hurry up before all the hot water was gone. Simultaneously the phone rang, and her head started hurting again. It took so little to overwhelm her. "Should I answer it?" she whispered. She heard the ringing stop, and the nagging feeling subsided. As she stepped out of the shower she faced a mirror clouded over from the steam; once again she was relieved, not quite ready to look at herself. The stabbing pain every time she moved was enough. She could see her legs and arms covered with superficial scratches and a nasty bruise on her inner thigh. But it was her back; the long cut on her back was definitely infected. It throbbed, and nearly took her breath away when the hot water hit it. She wrapped a towel around her long dripping hair then slipped on her robe; it felt warm and comforting.

"Where am I going to get antibiotics?" she muttered to herself. Walking out into a dark front room she did not turn on any lights until all the shades were pulled, doors and windows locked securely. She turned on a small lamp in the corner and sat down next to the answering machine that was incessantly flashing a red light.

"I don't want to listen," she whispered. "Thank God aunt Audrey is not here." She walked over to French doors that led out onto a patio. She turned the lock opening the doors, and stepped out to a wooden deck. The sound of the ocean waves lapping against a sandy beach with full moon overhead shining down on her face was soothing to her. She closed her eyes, took in a deep breath, relished the freshness of the air, and began to cry. Her shoulders shook as she placed her aching head in her hands, dropping down to her knees she continued to cry, salty tears stinging the cuts on her lips and face. The ringing phone silenced her crying, but again she chose not to answer. The machine came on and she could hear a male voice begging her to answer the phone. She remained still on the floor of the deck, lying down completely, and letting the sea breeze dry the tears on her face. She was so very tired. She closed her eyes falling asleep.

CHAPTER I

Jamie Ellen Blackstone, born June 1ˢᵗ 1977 in LaSalle, California has come miles to shed some of life's gentler moments and reach this point. Born to Mary Ellen Blackstone no longer among the living. At the time of her demise, Mary served spirits in a local tavern to patrons of the small western community lovingly called Gray Mountain, Montana. The name Gray Mountain reflected an immense mountain where the town sat directly at the base. The color gray in the name because of the never-ending steam from the river below rose up out to the trees, giving the mountain its' gray appearance. An undocumented condition of Mary's employment was to entertain a few of the town's wealthier gentlemen after closing each night in a back room of the tavern. All the while, Jamie lived in a large lush apartment upstairs conveniently made possible by a generous and grateful owner James Patterson, Mayor of Gray Mountain.

Jamie was well cared for. Her mother loved her and was willing to do nearly anything to give Jamie what she needed to grow up in the style Mary was denied as a child. Mary Blackstone was a stunning woman. With flowing natural red hair, large brown eyes, a petite body, with ample breasts. She was a "head turner," to coin a phrase from James who loved everything about her, especially the business she brought to his tavern.

Jamie's mother Mary was killed near her 41st birthday by a bullet that lodged in her brain. The yearly summer carnival was in town and business boomed. Many new faces came into the tavern, some from the carnival, and some from surrounding communities there to take part in an event that everyone looked forward to.

No one really knew what happened. There were tales spun for years to follow. Two men with unfamiliar faces in the tavern that night were arguing. Suddenly one man stepped back, drew a gun and fired. The bullet as the story was told ricocheted off the stone fireplace mantel and entered Mary's right temple. She lived for 48 hours on life support never regaining consciousness and then died. The two men that fled the scene were not found. An intensive search went on for over a year, some of which was funded by an angry, sad James Patterson. Regardless of the lifestyle James supported for Mary he loved her deeply, and neither he nor his business recovered from her untimely death.

Jamie, now sixteen years old was in shock for weeks after her mother's death. It certainly felt like a horrible dream. She seemed to be led from moment to moment, house to house, room to room, never really believing this awful thing had happened. She made decisions that she could not remember. People hugged her giving her condolences that she could not feel or understand. She kept expecting to hear her mother call her name or feel her gentle arms around her supporting her, but only silence and cold cruel emptiness.

Jamie's father did not attend the funeral. She had barely spoken to him in the past sixteen years. He never seemed to want to talk to her or write to her. The checks came in the mail, the presents for birthdays and Christmas, but no pictures or talking, from the man she called her father.

Her mother did not speak badly of him, she just did not speak of him. It was like they came together to have a baby and then he disappeared. There was only one picture of the two of them together, only one of Jamie and her father when she was three months old. If not for that single picture she would not have believed this man was her father at all. She did not remember him holding her or playing with her. She could not even recall his smile. When Jamie would ask why he left Mary would always find a reason to change the subject or leave the room. At one point in her very young life, she began to ask questions. Many of her playmates had fathers, where was her father? The explanation she received was short and to the point, "he left, he didn't like family life, and needed to be with his mother."

The summer of Jamie's twelfth year, she went to California to visit her aunt Audrey. During the visit, she begged Audrey to tell her the story of the breakup. Audrey said simply, "he just left." "Your mother and father met here, actually." "Your father Victor Blackstone, comes from another world." "It is a world of business tycoons, politicians, jet-setters, who have too much money, and an inbred loathing for the simple folk who just get by." "At that time your Uncle Ralph had a deep-sea fishing business." "He was actually a guide for the rich and famous, who wanted to go out and catch a big fish in the ocean but didn't have a clue how to accomplish that task, and of course, didn't want the stinky messy job of either disposing of the big fish, or finding someone to stuff it." "Those people just want everything to magically happen." "You know, there is no mess, no problems, just there when they want it." "Ralph did immensely well for us helping and pleasing those people." "Victor just happened to be among a group, who had flown in from Virginia that year, and wanted to catch one of those big fish." "Mary was living here then." "She was only twenty-five and drop dead gorgeous." "Victor was mesmerized from the minute he saw her, he really went after her." "She didn't have a chance; she was swept right off her little feet."

"When mamma and daddy Blackstone heard he was seeing a commoner, they immediately flew out here, and forbid him to continue the relationship." "I suspect Victor had never been told no in his life."

"He was furious with his family." "They threatened to disinherit him if he continued to see Mary." "To make a long story short, they made good on their promise and he was out, without a dime."

"They were married and moved in with us for a while." "At first, it seemed not to matter." "I mean they were so much in love, they couldn't keep their hands off each other." "Victor worked with Ralph in the business." "He never complained, or seemed unhappy, and within a year, Mary was pregnant with you."

"Victor was not happy about that." "This was a great game, and he was having fun with it, but now a large dose of reality, and he didn't like it." "Mary, however, was thrilled and was not quiet about that fact at all." "From that time on the fun was over." "The distance between them grew with each passing month." "When you were born, for a short time your dad seemed pleased." "You know, he actually acted like the proud papa." "Your mom and dad moved into their own little house down by the beach." "A cute little place, Mary had it all fixed up."

She paused staring at the floor. Jamie jarred her from her thoughts, "what happened after that?"

"Their relationship was never the same." "It seemed like your mom was trying so hard to make Victor happy." "He grew more and more indifferent to everything in his life." "He began to drink too much, they would fight, and it became an unhealthy environment for you." "Mary left you here at our house many nights when they were fighting," "She would always come back to pick you up; most of the time she was crying." "She loved him but did not know how to reach him." "He didn't beat her or anything like that but he was miserable, and seemed trapped, like a wild animal."

"One day there was a knock at my door." "I was dumbstruck when I opened it and there stood his mother." "Old Mrs. Blackstone herself, ugly and mean." "She didn't want to see you or Mary, she just wanted to talk to Victor." "I told her how to get to the shipyard." "Ralph said, when Victor saw her he ran to her like a little schoolboy who'd been lost, then found by his mom." "He fell down on his knees and cried into her skirt like a child." "She took him with her that day; that was the last time any of us ever saw your father."

"Mary was frantic, out of her mind with worry." "She called constantly trying to reach him, but no one would talk to her except their butler who finally would just hang up on her when she would call." "God, it was an awful time." "Mary was so depressed, couldn't eat, or sleep, or care for you." "That is the only time I ever saw her turn the care of you over to anyone else." "It took nearly a year for her to recover enough to be a productive person again."

"Then one day, out of the blue, she came walking into my kitchen with this book. "You know, one of those tourist books with all the pretty pictures of faraway places to visit." "There was this picture of a little town in Montana, called Gray Mountain." "It was a really beautiful picture of the sun setting over the mountains, with the town in the valley." She said, "this is where we are moving to start a new life, just me, and Jamie."

"We tried to discourage her, warning her of the dangers, alone with a small child moving to this town where she didn't know anyone." "Good God, I couldn't believe it." "But, she had made up her mind, and no one was going to change it." "So, off the two of you went to Gray Mountain." "One of the first people she met was James Patterson when she walked into his bar to ask if there was any work." "She went to work for him that very afternoon." "He put her in touch with his personal lawyer who managed to get a handsome settlement out of your father."

"Your parents started talking a little about you on the phone after that." "Actually, became civil, distant but civil." "I really believe, if they would have met under different circumstances, more on the same social ladder it would have been good for them, and I mean a forever sort of thing." "But the way it was, Victor just couldn't let go of the life he grew up in, as well as knowing Mary would never be accepted by his parents."

"You know honey; this had nothing to do with you." "You know that don't you?" "I mean you weren't the reason they split, they would have anyway."

"I guess so," Jamie replied. "It sort of sounds like if she hadn't gotten pregnant and had me, they would have stayed together."

"No Jamie, remember, I said they were growing apart, even before you were born."

Most of the town's people were at Mary's funeral, no relatives attended. Mary and Audrey's parents were dead, from an unfortunate auto crash, shortly after Audrey graduated from High School. Audrey was attending to Ralph, who had suffered a massive heart attack a week before, and he was now home recuperating, his physician ordering no extended travel.

It was only two months later, that Jamie was told she would be moving permanently to Virginia. She objected vehemently, acting out every emotion she could muster, hoping it might help keep her in Gray Mountain. Even James Patterson tried to persuade the Blackstone family that it was best Jamie not be uprooted from familiar surroundings so soon after her loss. Aunt Audrey, of course, offered to take Jamie but to no avail. For the first time, the

Blackstone family wanted Jamie, but she did not want them.

At one point, Jamie ran away from home, with her horse Redman and a mere knapsack of belongings. It took Gray Mountain Search Team two days in the mountains to locate a tired defeated Jamie and horse. At that point the Blackstone's decided enough time had passed; Jamie would immediately be transported to the house of her Grandmother and Grandfather Blackstone. To appease this stubborn child, they would ship her horse as well.

CHAPTER II

On a rainy dismal Saturday morning, Jamie said a tearful goodbye to neighbors, teachers, friends, her home above the tavern, and Gray Mountain. Like the funeral, many of town's people turned out for her good-bye, after which, Jamie was transported to the nearest airstrip where a charted jet flew her to Richmond, Virginia.

Not much of the trip was memorable. She was completely alone and she felt it everywhere. No one smiled or greeted her; not the pilot, the co-pilot, nor the attendant.

The gate leading to the main house was headed by two huge stone pillars, with the name Blackstone written across the top in black iron. The ride from that gate, proved therapeutic, passing beautiful green pastures surrounded by white boarded fences. The pastures were dotted with dairy cattle, bay, and sorrel colored horses, some eating quietly and some running spiritedly through the grassy fields seeming to play a game of tag. This picturesque setting took Jamie's attention away from her misery. She rolled down the window briefly to breathe in the sweet scent of fresh mown grass and alfalfa.

As they pulled up in front of the Blackstone mansion, Jamie could hardly hide her reverence. The mansion seemed to cry out, "Tara, you've come to Tara!" It was a sprawling white old southern style dwelling. A charming lattice covered porch encircled the entire mansion with lush green flowering plants hanging from every corner. Large etched glass windows adorned the front entrance door on either side, as well as every rounded corner of the house. Terraces appeared just outside of every upstairs room; flower gardens, walkways, gazebos, small ornate stone fountains at every turn of the head.

Even Scrooge himself, could not help but be in awe of the stark tranquil beauty of this place. Jamie's immersion in her surroundings must have amused the chauffeur; when Jamie finally came back to reality she was gazing up into a grinning black face looking down at her holding the door to exit the limousine. "It's really sumpin, isn't it?" Jamie didn't answer, just slowly crawled out of the limousine and walked to the front door with the chauffeur lumbering behind her.

Reaching the entrance, the large door opened and a man stood before her in a black suit and tie. He nodded briefly, saying, "You must be, Miss Jamie." He didn't give her time to respond, but followed that semi-greeting with, "I'll show you to your room, Mum."

Jamie asked, "What is your name, sir?"

"Briton, Mum." Jamie knew this must be the Butler Audrey talked about. He was slight of build, graying, looking to be about sixty-five. His face reminded her of a bulldog, with every line turned down. It was obvious to her he smiled very little. "Charles will be bringing up your luggage Mum."

As Jamie followed behind Briton, they passed through the entrance under an enormous chandelier, and toward an arching staircase leading upstairs. Everything seemed to be brilliant white; the shining floors, draperies, and walls. It made the whole area seem immense. They made their way up the staircase toward a room at the end of the hall.

The hallway was different from the entrance, warm with large mahogany doors and woodwork. The carpet was thick and soft. Tapestry prints, colored gold, and maroon hung from the walls.

As Briton opened the door to what was now Jamie's bedroom she was charmed. The room was large, open, and full of light. The floors a burnished wood, a brass bed with a yellow and white lace bedspread covered in many pillows. The ceiling to floor glass doors seemed to magnify the light coming in. Delicate ornately carved tables sat on either side of the bed, one topped with a vase of lovely yellow roses. A matching armoire sat near the foot of the bed on the opposite wall. Bookcases filled with books, a television hid cleverly in an additional armoire, and a white marble fireplace.

Briton woke her from her trance stating, "dinner will be at six, in the main dining room, Mum." "It will be formal tonight; the madam is entertaining."

"Where is my father?" Jamie asked shyly.

"They are all attending a private horse sale, Mum." Jamie merely nodded her head as Briton turned to leave shutting the door behind him.

A moment later Charles knocked on the door to deliver her luggage. When Charles reached the door to leave he turned to say, "I hope you enjoy your stay, it's a pretty place, for a pretty young lady like you." The first kind word, since she had left home.

Jamie smiled, and replied, "Thank you."

"That is OK honey, I meant it," Charles added.

"How many people live in this house?" Jamie asked.

"Three peoples mam, four with you." "That doesn't count the help."

A voice could be heard in the distance, "Charles, I have work for you, now." Charles shrugged, "I have to go."

"My name is Jamie." He smiled, nodded and then turned to go.

It was obvious Briton was in charge of the help.

Jamie went to investigate her new abode further. The bathroom was as plush as the bedroom; marble sinks, shower, and massive bath tub. Crystal lighting, brass handles, and mirrors, china bowls full of perfumed soaps, white roses, and pearls of oil for the bath. The walls throughout were painted a light pastel yellow with white running boards and woodwork. The general appearance was one of femininity and warmth.

Jamie opened the glass doors and walked out on to the terrace. The view was magnificent. It took in the same green meadows, white fences, and horses that she saw on the drive to the mansion. In the distance, one could see the barns, bunkhouses, and a stream to complete a perfect picture.

Jamie wanted to hate this place. That is what she thought about on the trip here, how much she would hate being away from Montana. How could anyone hate this place? Her father must love her; look at all this beauty he supplied for her. With that thought, Jamie returned to her room to unpack and pick out the prettiest dress she owned. She would bathe and do her best to make herself appear as beautiful as her father remembered her mother.

The clock on the bedside table said 5:55. It was time to find her way to the formal dining room. Jamie took one last look at herself in the full-length mirror on the front of the armoire. The dress was one she had never worn. It belonged to her mother and was just a bit tight. However, it was flattering, and in the reflection of the mirror, she saw a much older girl.... a woman.

Jamie had piled her long chestnut brown hair on top of her head with two wooden chopsticks holding it neatly in place. She was wearing some makeup which she rarely did. The dress was red silk, knee length with a small standup collar trimmed in gold. There were tiny buttons down the front, and a seductive slit, a little too long trailing up her right thigh. Her emerald eyes were heavily lined in black. Long gold earrings hung in place, and ruby red lips the final touch. "Mom would be impressed," she murmured.

Jamie was not the striking redhead her mother had been, but her beauty was more evident with each passing year. She had an earthy natural look with full lips, large green eyes, and olive colored skin. Her eyelashes and brows were darker than her hair; coal black, thick and feathery appearing. She was larger in stature than her mother, broad shoulders with long strong legs. One of her most endearing qualities was her smile; it could melt the coldest of hearts. Her mother always told her, when she smiled she took no prisoners.

As Jamie descended down the staircase she began to get a sick feeling in her stomach. Was it fear, excitement, or was it an omen? Reaching the bottom of the stairs she was unsure which way to go. She heard voices down the hall and music; a woman's high soprano voice singing in Italian. Jamie stopped momentarily closed her eyes listening to the sweet clear sound of the woman's voice. It was lovely, it made her feel elegant and refined. She moved toward the sound. Just before reaching the room in which the music was coming from, a man's voice startled her. "Miss Jamie?" She turned to see Briton staring at her with a quizzical look on his face.

"Yes, I was just coming for dinner," she replied quickly. He stood for a moment, looking at her a bit too intensely. He seemed to want to say something to her but couldn't quite come to it.

Instead, he replied, "Let me announce you." They walked into a large study filled with several people. Briton announced, "Miss Jamie Blackstone." The conversation died immediately as all turned to look at her. Jamie smiled at them, but the group seemed to be frozen in place gazing at her.

Finally, a tall gray-headed statuesque woman stepped forward. She walked up to Jamie and took her hand. The woman's hand seemed cold and weak; it appeared an effort to greet her.

"Jamie, so nice you finally arrived." "I am Sophia Blackstone." Jamie was staring into the face of her paternal grandmother, and she didn't like it. Everything about this woman was like ice. Her eyes, her hair, her skin color, seemed pale and cold. "Did Briton not tell you, to dress for dinner, not a party?" Jamie could feel her face begin to flush. "Well, I suppose you can't be expected to know any better." "This is most likely what your mother wore every night."

Quickly, rage began to build. Jamie wanted to tell her she looked like the walking dead, but before she could utter a sound her father appeared through the door of the study.

"Mother, mother, now let's not be witchy." "She is beautiful, isn't she? "No one in this room can come close but look whose daughter she is." He laughed easily, as he took Jamie's hand, and kissed it. She recognized him from the photo she had. He appeared a little older, but dark and strikingly handsome. He smelled of strong whiskey, and tobacco.

She realized she looked like him; the olive skin, green eyes, even her dimples were there. He was tall like his mother but stocky and firm. He seemed to exude warmth and charm. She felt the rage melting away as he marched her around the room to meet all the guests.

"Victor, I am sure the child is tired from her journey and would like to eat and retire early," Sophia said stiffly.

"No, I'm not." Jamie retorted. Victor laughed loudly slapping himself on the face and announcing, "she doesn't just look like me, she has my arrogance as well." One could almost see the cloud of smoke that rose from Sophia's persona.

"Really Victor, you could show some dignity," Sophia retorted.

Jamie was feeling strong and confident, holding tightly to her father's arm, so she smugly replied, "I didn't know dignity and rudeness were one in the same."

The room was deathly quiet as Sophia turned slowly on her heel toward Jamie. As Jamie looked into her face, she could feel her confidence drain from her body. Like someone had pulled a cork out of one foot, and at any moment she might have completely drained out onto the floor. The look on Sophia's face was one of intense hatred. Not anger, but utter unwavering hatred of her. Jamie could feel it pierce her very soul and she shrunk from it. Looking up to her father for support, she saw another dark sober face looking back at her with contempt.

Ice seemed to hang on the words that came from Sophia, "Jamie dear, I realize you might be a bit stressed right now, I am sure you are still grieving but I would like a word with you alone if you don't mind." Again, Jamie looked back up to her father; he nodded toward Sophia as if to say "go on." He had dropped his grasp of her arm to stare at her with total indifference on his face. Sophia led the way to a study off the dining area. As Jamie stepped through the door, Sophia closed it.

"Jamie, make no mistake about it, I am the mistress of this house." "You of all people, including the servants will show me total and complete respect, or I will send you packing and I will keep that plug you call a horse for what food and lodging you have received here." "Is that completely understood by you?" Jamie knew her face must shine with a red glow because she could feel the heat.

With that, she reopened the door and firmly stated, "come along now." For a moment Jamie thought she might cry and run from the room. Again, everyone turned to stare at her and Sophia. The silence in the room was broken by a deep booming voice stating, "well what has happened here?" "I leave the room for a few minutes, and the conversation falls completely off." Jamie turned slightly toward the sound of the voice. What she saw was a large older gray-haired version of her father. "Is this our new young member?" He was looking fondly at Jamie, then at his son, then his wife. No one answered. "Well then, it is obvious to me, if no one else is smart enough to escort this beautiful young woman to dinner, I shall."

Jamie remained statue-like unable to move on her own. Her grandfather Blackstone however, seemed to glide her through the air without her feet ever touching the ground. He led her into an adjoining room and in the center, was a formal dining room table at least fourteen feet long, and the largest chandelier Jamie could have ever imagined hanging over it.

Chester Blackstone seated Jamie to his right and then seated himself close to her at the head of the table. The remainder of the group slowly meandered in and seated themselves as well.

Jamie wanted to study the other people at the table. That actually had been a plan of hers before the evening had become a bust. Now she just wanted to sit quietly with her head down, suffer through dinner, and retreat to her room where she was going to cry all night.

But Chester Blackstone was not going to let her. The questions followed one on top of each other. "Was your trip in comfortable, Honey?" "How do you like the Blackstone Ranch?" "Is your room suitable for you?"

Jamie kept the answers, short and respectful. Not until Chester talked of Redman, did he finally engage her in conversation. "That's a fine-looking horse you brought with you, Honey."

"Redman?" Jamie responded with some surprise.

"So, that is his name, Redman." "Yes, an appropriate name with that deep red color of his coat." "He's a good looking one, friendly too." With this Jamie looked Chester in the face and smiled the warmest sweetest smile she could muster. She could visually see Chester melt like warm chocolate in the sun.

"I should have expected a beautiful girl." "Beautiful women traditionally always ride handsome horses."

Jamie, out of mere curiosity looked at the other faces at the table to see reactions to the intimate exchange that was going on between her and her grandfather. Her father's face was hard to see buried in his hands like his head hurt. Sophia stared at her wine glass with the same ugly intense look that was there during her dressing down of Jamie. The remainder of the people sat staring at Jamie and

Chester with open blankness; like they were waiting for the second feature and were not sure what to expect.

Only one, a handsome gentleman with sandy colored hair was smiling at them. "Chester said to him, "Jim, have you taken a look at Jamie's horse, Redman?" "The deep sorrel, with white mane and tail," Chester continued, "and four white socks?"

He responded with a sort of clipped cockney accent. "Yes, yes, that's the one." "I saw him at a distance, would like to look further though." "Is he for sale?"

"No!" Jamie responded quickly. Chester threw back his head and laughed hard,

"Well Jim, there's your answer."

"Where's he from?" Jim asked gently.

"Gray Mountain, Montana," Jamie said.

"Was he from Bob Jenkins herd?"

"Why yes," Jamie said excited just to hear a familiar name. "How do you know him?"

"If he deals in horseflesh, then I know him."

"You see Jamie," Chester said, "Jim Donaldson here, is most likely the most famous horse trader in the United States, Canada, Europe, and Australia." "He graciously works for us, as he does many others finding good horses for our ranch and marketing a bit for us on horses we want to sell."

"You flatter me Chester, my old friend," Jim responded. "But to get back to Bob Jenkins, he has good stock so I am sure your horse is a good one Miss Jamie," Jim said smiling.

"Have you been to Gray Mountain?" Jamie asked. "Many times, it is beautiful up there." "A bit cold in the winter but makes for hearty folk."

The warmth of the conversation was broken by the serving of dinner. Briton and a small Mexican girl, who looked to be around twelve or thirteen served the meal of stuffed Cornish game hens, various dishes of vegetables, fruit salads, homemade bread, and baked flan with caramel sauce for dessert. What Jamie ate of the meal was delicious.

Sophia began talking about a charitable ball that would be held in Richmond at the Governor's Mansion next month. She would be making some of the arrangements and were there any suggestions for musicians?

At that point, the conversation including Jamie died out completely as Chester loudly volunteered his ideas on what would be appropriate for the Ball. For the remainder of dinner, Jamie sat quietly, ate what she could, and asked to be excused shortly after finishing.

As she was leaving the room, she heard Sophia say, "Jamie tomorrow is Saturday, and we will be attending the races in town." "Please sleep in as long as you like, get acquainted with the ranch, perhaps you might like to ride your horse." "We shall return around six, and dinner will be at eight." "We will expect to see you then." There was a definite attempt at being cordial in her tone. Nevertheless, coolness hung in the air as Jamie retreated to her room.

After ripping off all her clothes, the chopsticks out of her hair, and washing off any traces of the makeup, she walked out on the terrace and let the wind blow through her hair. It seemed to be cleansing her of the pain she felt from her experience with her new family. She could hear the distant whinnies of horses. She felt the softness of the wind gently blowing, and the sweet smell of freshly mown hay. The sky was lit up with its bright star constellations, and a large half-moon.

She was exhausted, leaving the terrace doors open Jamie crawled into bed, continued to stare at the sky, and listen to the night sounds as she fell asleep.

Jamie was not sure if it was the voices or the light that woke her. She slid out of bed and made her way out unto the terrace. Looking over the railing she could see a group of men gathered around a large truck carrying hay bales destined for the barn. The men seemed to be enjoying themselves, slapping each other on the back, and spitting on the ground. One among them seemed busy counting the hay bales and instructing the others where exactly the bales were to be distributed. Jamie moved as close to the railing as she could get, so she could see him better.

He was young, medium height, with a shock of blond hair falling over the forehead of what appeared to be a handsome face. His arms were muscular and tan rippling as he adjusted the heavy bales. His physique tapered to narrow hips, apparent through tight low-cut jeans.

In her intense concentration on the young man, she failed to notice the others had noticed her and were pointing up at her. With their attention now all on Jamie, the young man could not help but notice what they were pointing at. He looked directly at her as she quickly backed away from the railing.

She could hear the erupting laughter from the group as she shut the doors.

She stood staring through the glass, as a knock at the door startled her. It was Briton holding a silver tray, "thought you might like a spot of tea, and perhaps a muffin for breakfast, Mum."

"Thank you", she replied as she took the tray.

He stood staring at her, again like he wanted to say more, but didn't know how.

"Was there something else?"

"Were you planning to do anything in particular today?"

"Yes, ride my horse," she replied curtly.

"Very good Mum, Ronald will help you at the barns."

"Who?"

"Mr. Ronald Bates, Mum." "He is the caretaker of the horses Mum."

"All right Briton, I'll look for him at the barns." She wanted to shut the door. She had an urgency to urinate, and she really didn't like this little man. He made her uncomfortable.

Jamie dressed in her favorite blue jeans, slightly worn, comfortable and form fitting. She also wore a brown leather vest that Mr. Patterson had given her for her last birthday. In addition to brown leather boots to match, she wore a simple white tee shirt under the vest and tied her hair back with a white scarf. She looked at herself in the mirror of the armoire; she looked her age and that suited Jamie's mood today. She wasn't interested in impressing anyone except the one who loved her, Redman, no one else.

She hurriedly made her way down the stairs through the front door, running headlong into Charles. "Here, here, here, where are you going in such a hurry child?"

"Oh, I'm sorry, I'm going to see my horse and I am in a hurry, I've missed him."

"It's OK Honey, you don't have to pologize to me." "You been missin your old friend like anyone would, so you go on and see him."

Now, Charles she liked, a sweet honest man bossed around by that little prick Briton. Wasn't that always the way with us common people, Jamie thought to herself.

The barn was a distance from the house, she enjoyed the walk. She stopped to watch two small foals playing next to the mares. Spotting Redman in the far corral she hurried on to the barn entrance. She found her way to the back-corral gate and whistled for Redman. The big red horse with white mane and tail, snapped his head up straight, seeing Jamie he ran toward her. She jumped over the fence to greet him, wrapping her arms around his muscular neck, scratching his ears, stroking his forehead and silky soft nose. Relishing in his smell, and the guttural sounds he made as he nuzzled her hand with his upper lip.

"Well, he seems to like you!" The voice made Jamie jump, as she turned quickly to see who was behind her. A young boy about ten years old stood smiling at her. He looked to be Latino or Puerto Rican.

"Hi, who are you?"

"My name is Raul, what is yours?"

"Jamie Blackstone."

"My sister works in the kitchen, have you met her?" "No, but I think I saw her for a moment last night at dinner," Jamie replied and was amused by this boy's enthusiasm.

"Her name is Teresa." "We came from Los Angeles with our father to work for Mr. Blackstone." "Where is your Mother?"

"She died last year of some kind of flu."

"I'm sorry to hear that."

"How is it your father came here?" "Well, Mr. Donaldson........."

"Raul, what are you doing?" "You are supposed to be getting oats for the trainers."

Jamie turned to see who was speaking. She came face to face with the blond man she was watching from the terrace that morning. He was so handsome, she was speechless. Strength and virility seemed to exude from his very being. He tipped his hat slightly, "excuse me, but just who are you?" Jamie was a little taken back by his tone.

Before she could answer, Raul blurted out "She's Jamie Blackstone, Ronnie."

He tipped his hat slightly again, only this time smiling, "so the long-lost daughter is found." Jamie was now openly irritated.

"No, I was never lost, I was not found, I was dragged here against my will!"

"Wouldn't we all like to be dragged to a place like this against our will," he said with acerbity.

Jamie pointed her nose in the air, "excuse me, I'd like to ride my horse now."

Sensing her obvious disdain for his remarks, he lowered his head and uttered in a low voice, "I'll saddle him for you."

Jamie responded a little louder than she meant to, "please don't bother; I'd like to do it myself." "As a matter of fact, I don't want anyone caring for Redman but me."

The glare in his eyes indicated he was now also irritated. "Right, I can just see you out here shoveling horse shit."

"I happen to like the smell of horse shit!" Jamie snapped back. "Now if you don't mind, where is the tackle room?" He didn't answer, just pointed toward the back of the barn.

She led Redman toward the barn and out of the corner of her eye she could see Raul attempt to follow as Ronnie grabbed his back belt-loop, lifting him off his feet.

Reaching the tackle room, she took a deep breath, "God, did I even breathe while I was out there?" Jamie said out loud to herself. She was definitely aroused by that little exchange. She could feel the heat in every part of her body.

She found Redman's blanket, saddle, and bridle. Quickly, she expertly prepared him for the ride, then bolted out the back door of the barn racing along the fence line and over the hill of the pasture not knowing where she was going, just riding. She could feel that eyes were staring at her, which made her flip her hair in the wind leaning closer to Redman. "Eat the dusty manure, Ronnie" she muttered out loud smiling.

Ronnie Bates was smiling too, as he watched her gallop off. He too muttered something under his breath, "little rich bitch."

She rode as far as she could go in one direction turning at the fence line, going as far as she could in that direction. The ranch was enormous, and she did not reach the other fence line before dark. Jamie and Redman galloped up hills, walked across pastures, waded in the creeks and river. She even lay in a meadow of wildflowers napping in the afternoon sun as Redman grazed. She really hadn't felt this relaxed since before her mother died.

By the time she returned it was very dark, and she had no way of knowing how late it was. As she approached the barn she could hear voices, loud voices. She quietly dismounted and tied Redman to the board fence. She slowly walked toward the back of the barn catching a glimpse of her grandfather shaking his fist in Ronnie's face. "I told you, she wouldn't even let me saddle the horse, let alone tell me where she was going."

"What kind of man are you, to let a little girl push you around like this, you son-of-a-bitch?" "We don't even know where to start to look!"

Jamie answered, "You won't need to." Chester dropped his fist from Ronnie's face. They both looked at her with angry expressions.

With stern authority, Chester stated, "What do you mean scaring us like this?"

"I didn't," Jamie responded lightly, "I just rode my horse, on your land I might add." Chester's face was beet red.

"Didn't Sophia tell you what time we would eat?"

"Yes, but I didn't have a watch."

Chester's eyes were slits as he angrily shouted, "if you ever pull this again you won't have that horse long."

Jamie's response was quick and furious, "if you ever take my horse from me, I will kill you!"

Chester dropped his hands at his sides, straightened his stance, and widened his eyes. Jamie stood defiant, while Ronnie looked like someone had just smacked him in the face.

It was silent, in an ominous way. Chester turned without saying a word and walked from the barn toward the house. Jamie had not moved an inch. She wasn't even sure she could walk, her legs felt numb. She continued to stand in the same spot, watching Chester walk up the hill. It was Ronnie who broke the silence.

"I have been here for six years; I have seen that man as mad as you would ever want to see a man." I've seen him stand up to powerful men, mean wild horses, even that ball-busting woman he is married to and he never backed down, or showed any sign of weakness." "What I just saw you do to one of the strongest men I have ever known makes me want to puke." "You are some kind of........." With that he turned and walked into the adjoining office off the tackle room, slamming the door behind him.

Jamie still had not moved an inch since her confrontation with her grandfather. Did Chester really care about her, or was this just a Blackstone control issue?

Ronnie had managed to deflate her ego and make her feel like the bitch he wanted to call her.

She walked to Redman, who was trying to catch a wink of sleep. "Poor baby," she cooed, as she rubbed his neck. She led him into the barn, removed the saddle and bridle, and then began brushing him down, the whole time watching the office for any sign he might come to apologize to her. There was no movement from the office.

After turning Redman loose in the corral, Jamie returned to hang up the saddle, and bridle, once again looking to the office for any sign of movement; she slowly made her way back to the house.

The door was unlocked leading to the kitchen galley. Her stomach was growling and gurgling, she was hungry. She tip-toed to the refrigerator and peeked in. There was a virtual smorgasbord of leftover goodies from dinner. Roast beef, fried chicken, cheeses, and desserts.

Jamie was happily munching on a chicken leg when a voice startled her.

"Can I help Senorita?" Looking back, she saw the small Mexican girl who helped Briton serve dinner the evening before.

"I am Jamie Blackstone; your name is Teresa, isn't it?" "I met your brother Raul down by the corral today." The girl didn't answer right away. She seemed to be speechless, unable to gather her thoughts enough to reply, so Jamie tried again, "I remember you from dinner last night."

"Si," she responded, and stepped back putting her head down.

"Listen, I am very hungry, you don't mind if I take a little food to my room, do you?" "I'm sorry I missed supper, I just lost track of the time and........."

Before she could finish, the girl was violently shaking her head saying, "Oh no, oh no, Senorita, I do this, let me fix for you." Jamie reached out for the girl's arm, and she recoiled like she had been bitten by a snake.

"It's ok, I can just throw a few things in a paper towel, that way there won't be any dishes for you." The girl looked like she might cry.

"No, no," she kept shaking her head. Jamie reluctantly gave in and sat quietly as the girl made her food on a silver tray, then followed her subserviently.

The little girl placed the food on Jamie's bedside table, and then hurriedly left the room.

"Wow, the poor thing, she acts like a slave," she said softly to herself.

She turned on her television, sat on her bed devouring the food prepared for her. Watching the television mindlessly, she could not stop thinking about what had taken place in the barn. The look on Chester's face as he turned to go to the house, the angry words spoken by Ronnie and most of all the driving urge to rip that man's tee shirt off so she could look at his chest. God, he was so exasperating, and yet so desirable. It bothered her that he had the opinion of her he apparently had.

Her thoughts drifted back to Gray Mountain, to the first time. The first time Jamie had ever really known what sex was all about. Last summer, Jamie then fifteen years old, working at the Stardust Drive-in as a car hop three nights a week, met a young man also working part-time at the drive-in as a cook.

John Wald, home from college for the summer, became one of her best friends. They seemed to hit it off the first time they met. Having many of the same interests, and philosophies, they would talk for hours about where each was going with their lives.

The attraction grew throughout the summer, kissing progressed to touching, and caressing, that progressed to red-hot unprotected sexual encounters, anywhere, everywhere they could find time alone. They grew more daring, and experimental with their play until they were caught red-handed by the local sheriff's deputy behind the main square's Fountain of David.

The deputy, of course, felt it his duty to inform both Jamie and John's parents. The humiliation ran deep, angry words were exchanged, and Jamie saw just how furious her mother could get. She was grounded to her residence for the rest of the summer, she was made to quit her job, as well as do menial labor for Mr. Patterson and her mother.

John's father was slightly put out by his son's actions, mostly to put on a good show for John's prudish mother, then slapped his son on the back and winked at him. No one, however could keep Jamie and John apart for the rest of the summer.

They managed to find each other discreetly in the shadows whenever possible until John left for college again.

What seemed so strange to Jamie to this day, was how that all ended. The relationship was so hot and sensuous, yet saying goodbye was relatively easy. They saw each other a few times after that. They remained friends and had one encounter when he was home on break, but they both knew it was over.

Jamie smiled to herself thinking of it all, she felt hot, sexy, and she wished John was here right now.

The noise from outside broke into her naughty dream world; loud voices and laughing. She walked out onto the terrace, from where she could see the circular front drive, a white limo parked with two finely dressed ladies, and her father standing beside it apparently drunk, apparently saying adieu, with poor Charles trying his best to herd her father toward the house, while attempting to convince the ladies to get back in the vehicle and leave.

It was infuriating to see him acting like a fool. She gritted her teeth, clenching her fists as she watched the sad scene unfold.

Charles persuaded the limo driver to help him direct Mr. Blackstone to the servant's entrance, most likely so there would not be a confrontation with Chester.

Jamie stood staring after the limo as it pulled away, catching sight of a movement in the shadows. A figure stepped forward, walked to the fence line, lit a cigarette, and looked off in the distance at the receding tail lights of the limo. Jamie recognized the figure to be Ronnie. She knew he had watched the whole affair with her father, she also believed he had been watching her but she did not believe he knew she had spotted him.

With all the anger she was feeling against her father, the sexual feelings she had been having just prior to this, she stepped closer to the terrace railing so the moonlight showed her image, and removed her blouse, jeans, then her undergarments.

She climbed up onto the railing, lying back, silhouetted in the moonlight, she knew he was watching her, and she felt charged with energy, as she lay naked, inwardly believing she was paying her father back for his injustice to her as well as her mother.

Concentrating so hard on her thoughts and feelings at first, she didn't hear the voice, "Miss Jamie, is that you?" "Are you all right child?" The instant she registered the sound of the voice, she knew it was Charles. She leapt from the railing leaving her clothes behind, slamming the terrace doors, and retreating into the bathroom.

Ronnie was in pain, and a bit embarrassed when he knew he had been noticed by Charles staring at a naked Jamie Blackstone. He walked toward the barn, feeling the pain of the huge erection he had acquired, that did not want to subside. "What the hell did she think she was doing?" "Was she crazy, or weird?" She was rapidly becoming an enigma to him, shaking his head, but damn it she really turned him on. Of all the women he had met for a while, she really made him hurt. "Why the hell did it need to be her?" "If he touched her, Chester would kill him." "He would hang me up by my dick, and stuff my balls down my throat," he said out loud.

CHAPTER III

Ronald Clearwood Bates, twenty-four years old was born in Laramie, Wyoming, a ranch hand's son. Actually, Ronnie did not know who his real parents were. He was abandoned by his mother on the steps of a ranch one spring morning with a note attached to his basket. Something about not being able to care for her son, hoping someone would take pity on the lad and take him in.

The sole proprietor of the ranch was eighty-five-year-old Betsy Maddox. She felt terrible for the infant, however, could barely care for herself with the help of her housekeeper, cook, and ranch hand. She hated to turn him over to the authorities; so cute, and sweet. She had no children of her own, only stepchildren from a marriage to her beloved Tristan whom she had lost to cancer years before.

They cared nothing for her, never visited, never called, it might not be bad to go out of this world with new life on the ranch.

Betsy knew she would need the help of her trusted ranch hand and friend, Steven Bates. He had worked for Betsy since he was a boy. He was a good, hard-working, decent man, married to a full-blooded Cherokee Indian woman, who was Betsy's cook and housekeeper.

They weren't just her employees; they were her family and would inherit all she had when she passed on. She had an ironclad Will written by her lawyer; she didn't want any of those selfish stepchildren thinking they had a right to anything that Tristan and she owned together.

The abandoned baby became Ronald Clearwood Bates, son of Steven and Chiwa Bates. Steven and Chiwa were no-nonsense people. Ronnie was taught from the very start that he should strive for achievement through tireless work, strength, and good virtues, not fame and fortune. Ronnie loved and respected his adoptive parents. He obeyed the rules set forth by his parents and loved Betsy like the sweet old grandmother she was.

However, life for Ronald was not happy, nor satisfying, but rather turbulent. There was an inward rage against the parents who abandoned him; a feeling that something important was always missing. No matter where he went or what he did, he ached inside. As he grew in stature, so did the rage grow in his heart and mind.

Rage came out directed at other peers in school, particularly those who appeared to have it all and flaunted it. The first serious episode happened on the playground in the fifth grade. A harmless game of touch football turned into a fistfight between him and a larger boy who had snatched the ball away only because he thought he could. The fight ended abruptly when Ronnie picked up a large fallen limb, smashed the boy in the face, then stepped over him as he lay bleeding in the dirt and walked home.

Even though the lectures were long, the punishment great Ronnie stayed in trouble most of the time acquiring a reputation as a bullying no-account, frustrating his parents as well as inflaming the local authorities who predicted his doom on a regular basis.

The final blow that nearly sent Ronnie packing off to reform school was Junior High prom night. He was actually escorting the prom queen who he had been dating for over a month.

Ronnie was seldom turned down by the girls. With his rugged good looks and polite mannerisms, he was popular. If a date did fall through it was usually because a parent discovered who their daughter was dating and forbid it.

The other males detested his existence. He was not a team player in anything; he was a loner, a tough guy, and a Romeo on top of it all.

Mid-way through the prom, Ronnie and Jane walked outside for fresh air, and a bit of romance. From out of the darkness came four figures. They grabbed him, drug him into the shadows with Jane screaming after them and beat him within an inch of his life using pipes, and a ball bat. By the time the teachers found him, he was unconscious; his face and head a bloody pulp. He did not regain consciousness for several days. His cognitive abilities were questioned, and the prognosis for complete recovery poor, but Ronnie prevailed.

Seventeen days out of the hospital two of the boys came up missing. Ronnie was arrested within hours, but not a trace of the boys could be found. Because of the lack of evidence, the authorities could not hold him. The animosity against him in the township was strong; he was advised to leave and not come back.

In the midst of all the turmoil concerning Ronnie's arrest, Betsy suffered a massive heart attack then died within hours. After the burial, the reading of the Will was held at the ranch. Surprisingly, the stepchildren did not make an appearance at the funeral or the reading of the Will. Betsy made good her word by leaving Steven and Chiwa the ranch. They inherited over thirty-five thousand acres of prime land, all of her personal possessions, and close to a million dollars in cash holdings. It was enough to increase their stature in the eyes of the town's people and authorities.

They hired a tutor from Laramie to help Ronnie finish high school. When not studying for graduation he was to help with the care, feeding, and training of the horses. The conditions were agreed upon with the local authorities. Ronnie was to stay on the ranch for one year, and if he left for any reason he was to be accompanied by an adult.

Ronnie was as good as their word. It seemed as long as he stayed away from others at the school there was no trouble at all. He was a hardworking, polite, soft-spoken gentleman.

The summer after Ronnie officially graduated he met Jim Donaldson at a horse auction in Bozeman Montana. Jim could see fine qualities in Ronnie, but he could see something else too. Like turbulent waters beneath a smooth surface, Ronnie had a deep foreboding quality about him, almost dangerous. Nevertheless, Jim highly recommended Ronnie for the new foreman job on the Blackstone ranch.

Upon meeting Ronnie for the first time, Chester immediately liked the young man. He was strong, intelligent, and self-assured. He wasn't just good with horses, he was phenomenal. He was quiet, but when he spoke he had something to say. The horses seemed to sense his love for them, yet he had a gentle firmness keeping them in tow.

Chester not only liked him he admired his qualities to a degree he found himself wishing Ronnie was his own son, rather than that mama's boy, Victor. He couldn't dwell on this type of thought long, or he would find himself drinking too much, and then driving to Richmond to spend a night with a real woman.

Erma Maples, even thinking the name made his groins ache. A lady of distinction in his eyes, but to Sophia and the rest of her fellow cronies, Erma would be a trollop, a harlot, a low-life, not fit to give a minute of time too. He chuckled to himself if she only knew how many times Erma held his head on her big plump breasts, or bed down with him giving of her generous body willingly. He loved her deeply, he often dreamed of making her his wife, wondering if he could get by with choking that prig Sophia, in her sleep. Then reality and guilt would overtake him, and the drinking would begin again. It was a vicious cycle.

Ronnie knew about Erma, he learned shortly after taking the foreman position at the Blackstone ranch. Ronnie received a phone call in the office of the tack room, from Chester requesting Ronnie to help him. He had wrecked his new Suburban and asked that Ronnie come alone, not telling anyone else of the accident.

When Ronnie arrived at the scene, Chester was sitting on the ground, a nasty gash across his forehead, the Suburban crumpled in a tree. Chester did not want the police called, asking Ronnie to take him to Erma's place, and then make the necessary arrangements; taking care of having the Suburban fixed, making restitution with the owner of the tree, most of all hushing the incident.

Without question, Ronnie did as he was told, and was rewarded with a handsome meal at Erma's the following evening. Ronnie sealed his friendship with Chester by making up a convincing story told to Sophia about a spirited unbroken horse that Chester encountered at one of the sale barns that lashed out and kicked him grazing his forehead. The Suburban was fixed so quickly she didn't even know it had been gone.

Ronnie had endeared himself to Chester. He took the place of the son Chester believed he did not have. He regretted not being able to openly give the luxuries to Ronnie he was capable of giving; to ease his own conscience, Chester would often slip a generous check into an envelope, and place it into

Ronnie's mailbox in the tack room office. At first, Ronnie protested, he felt deeply about his good fortune, finding work that only some could dream of. He was already wealthy by most standards, the only heir of Steven and Chiwa. However, wealth was not important to Ronnie Bates, and to Chester, that alone was a measurement of the quality of man Ronnie was.

Sophia, on the other hand, only tolerated Ronnie. He was an irritant, like a gnat flying around her head. He stayed far enough away so she was not often confronted, but he frightened her; like Chester did when he drank. She despised the way Chester would brag about him, the way he handled some damn horse. No matter what her dear Victor did, their own son, it was never good enough for Chester. Let some commoner put a saddle on a green broke colt, and it was a miracle.

Sophia secretly hated the horse ranch. She would never utter that to Chester, for fear he would start drinking again, then expect her to lay down while he groped and pawed calling it lovemaking. It had been a long dry spell, and she wanted to keep it that way. When life became unbearable in this smelly horse world, she would close her eyes tightly and imagine Chester dead, the ranch sold, and her with her son Victor living in one of the enormous Victorian mansions in Richmond. "All good things come to those who wait," she would whisper ever so quietly. That was what her Nana always told her, and she knew it was true.

CHAPTER IV

Since the confrontation with her grandfather and her display on the balcony, Jamie had been keeping a very low profile. She slept in until at least 9:00 each morning, knowing everyone would most likely be gone or too busy to notice her snatching bits of food from the kitchen. Every morning she raced out the door toward Redman.

Ronnie was usually doing chores, and even if he did notice her he looked another direction or hurriedly retreated into a building. The only living person she had any exchanges within more than a week was Charles. She chose to think he had not really noticed she had no clothes on that night and was just simply afraid she might fall from the balcony. He never mentioned the incident so neither would she. But he was a human voice, someone she trusted. When she would tire of riding horseback she would ride around the ranch with Charles on his little cart. At night if she was lonely, she would sneak down to his cabin by the creek and they would talk. She knew inwardly no one in the family would approve of this.

She certainly did not want to get her dear friend, her only friend in trouble so she was very discrete. They talked about horses, sports teams, and how they grew up. Charles reminisced fondly of when he was a boy growing up on his father's farm, and Jamie listened intently to his stories. Many of his ramblings were amusing and delightful. Jamie felt a warmth and a closeness to his man, she felt like she would trust him with her life.

One morning as Jamie came bounding down the staircase heading for the kitchen she ran straight into her father. She had not seen him since the limousine incident, and she was sure his last recollection of her would be the first night she was in the mansion.

Momentarily they stood staring at one another; he spoke first, "so you are still here," "I thought perhaps you had returned to beautiful Gray Mountain." His tone was demeaning and sarcastic.

Jamie knew at that moment it had been her grandfather who had sent for her. She felt hurt, anger, she wanted to fly at him, claw his face, put her arms around his neck and hug him, and hope he hugged her back. These feelings were foreign to Jamie, both love and hate intertwined. It left her feeling weak. "You would have known that I was still here if you had bothered to look, or even ask," she responded.

"It's no skin off my ass baby." "Come or go, I don't care."

"But you are supposed to care you are my father," Jamie said, almost begging.

"Look, let's get this straight." "I was not given a choice where you were concerned, I never asked to be a father, I never wanted to be one, not then, and not now!" "Got it?" His eyes glared coldly at her. He followed with, "the only reason my old man insisted that you come here to live, is he is going to make damn sure I am not the only heir to his millions."

Jamie's response was swift, "and I will make damn sure you are not!" His expression reflected so much hate she could not breathe. Oh God, she did not want this, why couldn't he just love her? She knew she must run, she just could not look at him a minute longer. She bolted past him and out the front entrance. She kept moving toward the corral in which Redman stood. She was sobbing as she wildly saddled him for her escape.

"Jamie?" she turned to see Ronnie. "What can I do?" he asked.

She needed to rid herself of some of this pent-up anger, "how about go to hell," she yelled.

She mounted Redman without looking back and streaked across the hill. She prodded Redman on, galloping until he seemed winded so she pulled him to a halt, dismounted, and lay down in the grass and continued to sob. Once she had quieted she lay silent thinking about her mother, her father, and his cruelty. She could not even fathom her mother ever loving someone like this.

It was getting dusk; she was tired and ravenous. She headed Redman back towards the barn. She wanted to walk slowly but he was having none of it. He obviously was anxious to return to his stall for oats and water so she allowed him to canter back.

When they approached the barn, Ronnie was waiting for them. She rode up to where he was standing. She starred into his eyes and saw concern. He placed his hand on her thigh.

"Can I help the lady down?"

She surprised herself by responding "yes."

He grabbed her waist as she dismounted, guiding her gently to the ground. She turned to face him with every inch of her body tingling. He reached up and stroked her hair, "just for tonight would you trust me to put Redman up?" "I think you could use some dinner, and a nice soft bed to lay your pretty head down on." She wondered at the softness in his voice, it made her eyes fill with tears. She quickly put her head down and stepped back from him. She was not going to break or let him see her cry again.

"I trust you with Redman any time." "I am sorry for the go to hell remark before and...."

"Jamie, please, it's fine, just go on to the house."

"All right, I am going." "Thank you for this." He nodded and led Redman into the barn.

She really didn't want to leave now; she wanted more of his closeness, far more. But she did as he suggested and slowly strode back to the house. Entering through the servant's entrance, she went straight to the pantry.

A crack of light was coming from the slightly open door; she peeked into what were Briton's quarters. What she saw revolted her. The small Mexican girl sat on Briton's lap, wearing only her thin white little nightgown; the outline of her naked body shown through the material. He was whispering something to her and running his ruddy fingers through her hair. She looked terrified and so small perched on his knee.

Jamie was ravenous, but now she was nauseated and horrified. She stepped back from the scene, in doing so she caught the edge of a pan sitting on the counter sending it to the floor with a loud bang. Briton jumped to his feet knocking Teresa to the floor. He flipped on the kitchen lights finding a panting red-faced Jamie.

Obviously irritated, he said, "Is there something you need Mum?"

"I came to get some food." "Dinner is over, but I will make something for you, mum."

"Forget it Briton, I have lost my appetite." "Who do you have in your quarters Briton?" His bulldog face was tight with frustration.

"That would be none of your business, mum."

"Really, well Briton, the last time I heard what you are attempting to do or may have already done is against the law." "Raul told me she is only thirteen that is rape Briton." "Maybe the sheriff would be interested, or my grandfather."

"No, no, no, Senorita, it is my fault." Teresa stood in the doorway, crying, shaking her head, and repeating the sentence over and over.

Briton turned to Jamie, smiling, "who did you want to call?" "I am not sure Teresa here, or her family's green cards are in order." "Do you really want to be the one to see this poor child sent back to an impoverished existence?"

Teresa's wailing seemed to grow louder with these statements, throwing herself down on the floor in front of Jamie, clasping her hands as if in prayer in front of the Virgin Mary. Jamie looked at the smug look on the bulldog's face. She stepped closer to him and hissed through clenched teeth, "regardless of what BS you have told this poor child, if I ever see you touch her again, I am telling my grandfather, and calling the law." With that, she jerked Teresa to her feet, "go to your father, now!"

Teresa ran from the room. Glaring at Briton, she took a piece of bread with a cola from the refrigerator and left the kitchen. Hurriedly she made her way to her bedroom. She stripped off all her clothes and then stood in a hot steaming shower in an attempt to wash away a feeling of uncleanness. Wrapping herself in a robe, she devoured the bread and cola. Once again, she went to sleep with the doors open, allowing the night sounds to lull her to sleep, "God, what a day." "Please let tomorrow be better."

CHAPTER V

Jamie was surprised when she awoke and found it was nearly 10:00 am. She quickly dressed, anxious to find out where her grandfather was. It was now very important to her to make amends with him. Not just because of the unfortunate statement, she made to her grandfather, but because she knew it was he who wanted her. He was living breathing flesh and blood that cared for her, and she was sorry she had hurt him. She had also appointed herself Teresa's guardian. She would win that little girl's confidence and watch over her; Briton will not touch her again.

That morning the house was eerily quiet. Teresa was nowhere to be seen, Briton's door was shut. The shades in the kitchen had not been opened. Jamie looked for something to eat, deciding to eat toast and fruit salad. She sat in the kitchen on a bar stool and watched the small television on the counter as she ate. Charles came through the door, smiling at her. She was glad to see him; it had been a couple of days since they had talked.

"Hey pretty girl, how you doin this fine mornin?

"I am good Charles, I am glad to see you, I missed you yesterday."

"Well, I was around Miss Jamie, but I didin see you."

"I was out on Redman all day."

"My goodness child, you gonna wear that big animal out."

She laughed out loud, "Oh Charles, you always make me laugh."

"Well, I'm happy I can make you have a happy moment."

"Listen, Charles, where is everyone?"

"Well Mr. Blackstone your grandfather, he's still in California, posed to be home tonight though." "The Mrs. is in town hiren more servants."

"Wait a minute, Charles, why is she hiring more?"

"Well, it's a funny thing but, little Raul, his sister, and father Michael left last night."

"What do you mean left?"

"Well, they just up and left, not a word to a soul."

"Where is Briton?"

"Yes, mam, he had to leave too." "Some close member of his family is sick." "So, he is gone too."

"The Mrs. was running round here like an old chicken with her head cut off this mornin." "No one to cook for her, she can't take that." "Youda thought the worlds a comin to an end."

Jamie had to smile at his words and antics, describing her grandmother. "So, do you think she'll have success?"

"Yes mam, she won't come back till she does." "She said, this mornin, no more foreigners, they are not reliable." "I just ain't believen that Michael would take his childrens and leave like this." "There's no reason that I know of."

He stood shaking his head in disbelief, as Jamie sat deep in thought. Briton warned them, God knows what reason he used to make them all run like this. They were obviously illegal. She had a hint of guilt that it was because of her outburst that this family left. But Teresa was better off, she might not know it now, but she was. Her grandfather would want some answers, and she was going to give them to him.

"Charles, can you give me a ride into town later, I want to do some shopping."

"Why certainly Miss Jamie, it would be a pleasure."

She walked to Charles wrapping her arms around his shoulders and hugging him tightly. "Charles, you are my good friend, you know that don't you?"

He hugged her back and patted her affectionately on the arms. "You a sweet sweet child, and I love you."

"Oh Charles, such a doll." "I'll see you out front in an hour, OK?"

"Yes mam, one hour."

Jamie needed to ready herself for her shopping trip, but first, she wanted to see Ronnie and Redman of course. After reaching the barn she looked everywhere for Ronnie and was disappointed when he could not be found. She quickly gave Redman his usual hug and ear scratching. Then she headed back to the house to ready herself for a trip to town.

Richmond was truly a pleasant surprise. It was charming with many quaint shops and stores. Charles seemed to know what would suit her best. She wanted feminine, conservative, and mildly sexy. She wanted to look her age, but with a look that states, she is for all intent and purpose a woman. Her goal was to impress her grandfather.

She spent her money freely, picking out each outfit carefully, planning each encounter strategically. When they reached the ranch, Sophia had already hired two more cooks and a stand-in butler. Two gray-haired ladies were scurrying around the kitchen preparing dinner. The butler was a tall slender noble-looking man, who smelled of alcohol and smiled all the time. Jamie was amused and for the moment felt very good and in control.

The butler had informed her dinner would be served at 7:00; she planned to be ready and there on time. The dress was basic black, simple yet refined. She wore a small diamond pendant and earrings to match. Her hair left down, no bands or ties, just long dark, and luxurious. She wore very little makeup, enough to enhance her large green eyes, and full sensuous lips. Again, she looked in the mirror of the armoire and liked what she saw.

She confidently walked down the long staircase, once again meeting her father at the bottom as he gulped down his third martini. She looked him straight in the eye and smiled as sweetly as she could "good evening father." She did not stop; she knew he was caught totally off guard. She headed for the den near the dining area where she could hear voices.

The butler was standing by the door, and turned to greet her, "I am sorry sir, I did not catch your name."

Still smiling, and still smelling of alcohol, "James madam, James is my name."

"Nice to meet you James, and please don't do one of those official introductions, everyone knows who I am."

"Yes mam, as you wish." He stepped back as she entered the room.

The only people there were Sophia, Chester, and two men she did not recognize. They turned as Chester stopped in mid-sentence when he saw her. She did not wait for a response, she walked directly to him taking his hand, squeezing it ever so gently, and softly saying "I missed you grandfather, where were you?" She followed this greeting with a beautiful smile.

Sophia then started, "well that is very sweet of you, but......" and was cut off completely by Chester,

"Sophia, shut up," if you ruin one more dinner with my beautiful granddaughter, I'm going to personally lock you in your room."

"Chester, my dear, this is not amusing our guests."

"Correction, they are my guests, not ours, and I am telling you, you will not embarrass Jamie tonight, do you understand?"

"Father, Father, where is your loyalty?"

"Are you talking to me, Victor?" "My lazy, alcoholic, ungrateful son who wouldn't know something valuable, or priceless if you slapped him in the face with it." "You shut the hell up as well, or I will just throw your ass out."

Jamie was enjoying this thoroughly but knew Chester had all the earmarking's of a man who had drunk a bit too much before dinner and really did not want a brawl on her behalf in front of these men.

"Grandfather, you have not introduced me to these gentlemen." Chester immediately stopped his attack and introduced Jamie to William Justin Davis the 1st, and his son Justin Fouche Davis, horse traders and ranchers from Mendocino, California.

Dinner proved interesting for Jamie; Justin falling all over himself, openly flirting with Jamie, and her own grandfather competing for her attention. All the while, Sophia, and Victor sulked.

Jamie stayed the exact amount of time she felt was appropriate, excused herself stating she was a bit tired and would retire early. All gentlemen with the exception of her father jumped to their feet at her exit, her grandfather kissing her hand, and wishing her a restful night's sleep. As she left the room, she smiled sweetly at Sophia and her father. It was perfect, just as she had planned. She could not have hurt them more if she had beaten them with a whip against their bare backs. But the night was not over yet.

It was nearly 11:00, and she was about to make a trip downstairs. She was dressed in a light pink negligee and robe; she looked soft as well as feminine. She made her way to the study. She knew she would find Chester there. Charles told her Chester spent many a night reading in the study, unable to sleep. She figured due to the chaos at dinner along with the drink, he would be spending most of his time in the study.

As she suspected, he was there, asleep in a chair, with his spectacles on and a book resting in his lap. She gently removed his spectacles; in doing so did wake him.

"Honey, what are you doing down here?"

"I should ask you the same."

"Sleep just doesn't come that easy, unless I am sitting up reading a book."

"That is not healthy for you, you know."

"So, do you care now?" "Before today you wanted to kill me."

"I'm sorry, I was upset just the thought of losing someone or something else I love sends me into a panic."

"Dear sweet Jamie, I am also sorry I should not have threatened you with the loss of your horse."

"Grandfather?"

"Please Jamie, could you call me Chester?" "The term grandfather makes me feel very old." "I've never heard that before you know."

Jamie laughed. "I'll be glad to call you anything you want if you will promise me something."

"And what is that dear?"

"That we could go somewhere or do something together sometime." He sat straight up in his chair, smiling.

"Jamie, that would make me a very happy man." "Would you allow me to plan a day for us, maybe tomorrow?"

"Oh, yes, grandfather... I mean Chester." "Could it include some horseback riding?"

"Absolutely my dear, how about first thing in the morning, before breakfast?"

"Wonderful, shall I see you at six?"

"Six, no let's do seven, I am too old for six." With that, they both laughed and hugged. "May I walk you to your room?"

"Why, of course, kind sir." As they left the room, neither of them noticed the shadowy figure in the darkness, watching them.

CHAPTER VI

The rest of the summer flew by and was so pleasurable the pain she felt from the loss of her mother lessened with each passing day. Nearly every waking moment was spent with Chester. He was proud to have her by his side; he made it apparent to everyone, especially Jamie. He escorted her to the races, parties, horse auctions, shopping for beautiful clothes and jewelry, as well as dining at many fine restaurants.

Chester took Jamie flying in the family-owned Lear jet, and deep-sea fishing with his friends. She basked in the warmth of his admiration and love, thus returning that love as openly as he. All walls she had erected around her for protection from the Blackstone's, had come crashing down, for Chester.

She told him the story of Teresa and Briton. Chester immediately alerted the authorities, much to Sophia's dismay. "Why can't you just keep your mouth shut Chester?" "She was just a little Mexican servant girl, and most likely is back in Mexico." Why expose our family to a scandal?" This produced ire from Chester, yelling obscenities at Sophia which always sent her fleeing to her room for asylum.

Sophia brooded, detesting Jamie's existence. She was the enemy, and she would be permanently eliminated if Sophia could just get by that stupid man. She hated Jamie with every thread of her being. She was a flirtatious, teasing, coy little bitch, who had managed to enamor every male for fifty miles around the ranch. That is except for her son, Victor. He knew what she was, a trollop like her mother and most likely not even Victor's child; a subject that had nearly driven Sophia mad. She thought of this each day of her life since she was told that Jamie was born. Because of her obsession, she had effectively driven Victor to serious drinking, demanding a paternity test nearly every day since Victor had returned to her. He protested each time, stating it was of no use he knew the child was his.

The only escape from the constant pressure of Sophia was to drink and stay inebriated enough to be oblivious to her incessant nagging.

When Chester left on business, Jamie stayed in her room, rode Redman, or traveled around with Charles on his cart helping him with his duties. Sophia despised this behavior most of all. In her eyes, this was an embarrassment to the family. No matter how much she loathed her, Jamie was still a Blackstone, and for her to be cavorting with the ranch hands and servants especially a black man, was inexcusable.

She tried to put a stop to it, but of course, Jamie immediately enlightened Chester, and he blasted Sophia using undignified foul words in front of the servants. He had humiliated her, and Jamie rubbed her nose in it, by associating even more with the kitchen help, and even the butler. The most distressing thing was they obviously loved her and seemed to show less and less respect for Sophia. She would find a way to rid herself of this little pest one way or another, after all, she had done it once before.

Jamie tried to spend more time near Ronnie, especially when Chester was gone. But every time the conversation seemed more intimate, and the warmth seemed apparent between them, he would pull away. She could not understand, and at times it would hurt her enough she would cry, when alone.

On a warm evening near the end of summer, she lay on the hay watching the sunset on the horizon. It was a beautiful evening. The stars gradually began to appear, crickets began to sing their abrasive melody, an occasional dog would bark in the distance or a horse whinny, and to add to a lovely evening, soft music was coming from somewhere. She closed her eyes and breathed in the sweet smell of the hay. When she opened them, Ronnie was standing over her, smiling. He startled her, but what a pleasant surprise.

She could feel the heat transcend through her body as he sat down close to her. "Must be some dream you are having."

"Why do you say that?" she answered meekly.

"Because you were smiling with your eyes closed and you looked so peaceful, and.... beautiful."

"How very sweet Ronnie, I was just enjoying this gorgeous night." "I hate to see summer end, don't you?" "Yeah, there is nothing like a summer night." He turned and looked at her longingly, deeply.

She was on fire. Jamie had never been this close. With his tough exterior, he had a boyish appearance up close; skin so smooth and tan. He had a small showing of light brown beard, a day's growth, full delicious lips, and eyes as blue as a new morning cloudless sky.

They moved together simultaneously, lips touching ever so softly at first, and then a bit more pressure growing in urgency as if they knew eventually the kiss would end, and neither wanted it to. The kiss ended and then led to another and another, each better than the first. She ran her fingers through his hair, knocking his hat to the ground. She touched his face, eyes, mouth, as he did the same to her. She was leading, he was following, and she wanted him; all of him.

This continued as she removed his shirt, marveling at his expansive beautiful chest. She played with his nipples, rubbed his arms, chest, and back; kissing, sucking, tasting every part of his male body. She removed her blouse, her bra, and pressed her breasts against him. He gently caressed and kissed her breasts, pulling her on top of him and at last, she could feel his hardness. She was ready for him to take her. Never had she needed to restrain herself from reaching orgasm, but she wanted to stretch this moment out. She pressed her own pelvis down onto his hardness, answering him.

Suddenly he stood up causing her to roll off him, onto the rough hay. "Ouch, what is wrong?" she asked, totally exasperated.

"Nothing Jamie, but I need to go now."

"What?"

"I am sorry", he said stuttering, "I promised I would do this job for Chester tonight, and I guess I forgot about it so I need to go now." He disappeared into the tackle room, shortly after which Jamie heard the truck start and watched the taillights quickly disappear.

She sat motionless still naked from the waist up. She was stunned, repeating to herself out loud, "what did I do?" After being bitten by insects, she dressed and returned to the house hurrying to her room, not wanting to talk to anyone. She showered, put on her robe, and sat on the floor at the end of her bed thinking over and over again about the happenings of the evening. Her feelings would ebb from ecstasy to agony remembering first the kiss, then his touch, and then his abandonment.

Ronnie drove the pickup a few miles from the ranch, then jumped out, walked to the back of the truck, and kicked the tires repeatedly. "Damn it, damn it, damn it, why her, God why her?" He loved her, and he knew it. He wanted her more than he had ever wanted any woman, but he couldn't have her, she was Chester's granddaughter, and he was nothing but a ranch hand; he wasn't worthy. With that, he drove to Erma Maples.

CHAPTER VII

Summer had ended, and fall was creeping into place. Chester enrolled Jamie in Mount Carmel, a private high school for girls. At first, she protested but changed her mind about its possible potential at the *Coming Out Party* Chester arranged for her.

Many of the girls who would attend the school were invited, along with their parents. Others included the school faculty, some friends, neighbors, the governor, and wife.

Symphony members were there to play their string instruments in the large front vestibule. Jamie wore a simple sheath, light gray, pin stripped, with lovely diamond earrings, a pendant, and bracelet to match. She wore her hair up in a simple style. Chester pranced around with Jamie on his arm, introducing her to everyone.

Mother Ann Saron was the Mother Superior at the school. Jamie liked her the minute she met her. She was warm and friendly, with a loud boisterous laugh.

Father O'Malley was equally as delightful. He was a round, red-faced, smiling, energetic gentleman, who obviously enjoyed Chester's company. He liked to tell Chester jokes. Each comic story was followed by thunderous laughter and a round of back pats.

Then there was Victoria Shelly, one of the young ladies' present at the party, and Jamie immediately bonded with her. Barely five feet tall, weighing less than 100 pounds, she made Jamie feel like a giant. She was also a virtual bundle of energy, vitality, and enthusiasm. She loved to take pot shots at the guest's by making clever comments about how they looked, walked, talked, and what they wore. Victoria kept Jamie laughing most of the evening, that is when Jamie was not being escorted by Chester to meet a new arrival to the event.

Victoria became Jamie's best friend and confidant. She was even privileged enough to be told about Ronnie. "Why don't you just march down to that tackle place and fuck him?" stated an impatient Victoria.

"I guess because I am as afraid of rejection as anyone else," replied Jamie.

"Bullshit, at least you will know if he cares at all."

"Believe me he cares, I will never forget that kiss and how it felt; believe me he cares." "He has to be avoiding me because he is afraid my grandfather will not like it." "I mean, that has got to be the reason," Jamie would say shaking her head wishing there was a way to reach him.

Jamie was instantly popular at school. Her studies came easily; she enjoyed her classes, her teachers, and most of all her new friends. She did not mind that it was a school for girls because thoughts of other males did not enter her head. Even when the girls talked of attractive male movie stars, musicians, boys around the Richmond area, her thoughts were filled with Ronald Bates. She could not forget that summer night, and how it felt.

Days past, and the school year was rewarding, filled with academic achievement, and warm friendships, especially with Victoria. A day did not pass without them conversing many times. Through it all Chester was never far away, sharing in her youthful exuberance. What time Jamie had to herself she managed to share with Redman and her many acquired friends around the ranch. She had become very popular with all the servants and ranch hands. She remembered all of their birthdays, shared in their joys and sadness. But the people she wanted to be closest to eluded her, Ronnie and her father.

She secretly wanted a relationship with her father but refused to allow him to recognize any weakness in her. She treated him openly with indifference, as he did her.

The relationship with Sophia became a game. A game she enjoyed and almost never lost. She openly flaunted her close bond with Chester knowing it was eating Sophia alive. When Chester was gone she stayed close to her friends on the ranch, especially Charles. Sophia hated Charles almost as much as she despised Jamie. First, he was black who Sophia considered inferior to her race, he loved Jamie which automatically made him an enemy and worst of all, Chester was fond of him, thus untouchable to Sophia. To cope with this impossible lifestyle, her time was spent with Victor when he was sober that is, and the time when he was sober seemed to dwindle with each passing month. She often went to Richmond to spend the day with women of her caliber, who lived the life she so wanted.

Jamie tried to see Ronnie as often as she could. He seemed to instinctively know when she planned to do so because he was inevitably gone when she had intended an encounter.

Ronnie ached inside, it was constant and merciless. At one point he considered confronting Chester with his love for Jamie, with a promise to always protect her and care for her. He knew she needed protecting. He was aware of the hostility toward her from Victor and Sophia. He considered Victor to be a non-threat simply because the majority of the time he was incapacitated and couldn't harm anyone if he tried.

Sophia, however, was another problem. She was mean and conniving, in addition, she had the money to buy someone to destroy Jamie, which in turn would destroy Chester. He worried about this every day. The other servants and ranch hands seemed to all share the same idea, particularly Charles. Charles and Ronnie often talked about this. They both worried for Jamie's safety and vowed to watch over her from afar, agreeing that approaching Chester was not the wise thing to do.

Being the young virile male that Ronnie was, he needed female companionship which Erma Maples supplied for him. Erma had a niece, Mary Lloyd. Mary was more than happy to supply Ronnie with anything he might need. Mary was not particularly visually attractive to Ronnie, as Jamie was. But she was a sweet girl, plump like Erma with generous breasts, a pretty face, and large brown eyes. She was a good listener, did not give unwanted advice and had an uncanny ability to know just what would please Ronnie; best of all expected nothing of him.

When Ronnie's frustration ebbed, it was Mary he went to. Chester knew of Mary and approved, believing Ronnie had the same point of view about Mary as he had about Erma. Chester had even taken it upon himself to gently lecture Ronnie on not waiting too long and losing a woman like Mary. Ronnie would listen with quiet respect inwardly wanting to tell him who he really wanted to spend his life with.

On Holidays, he would fly home to Wyoming to spend time with his parents. The whole time away from Virginia a fearful portentous feeling haunted him. He never stayed long in Wyoming.

CHAPTER VIII

"Why are your parents insisting that you do summer school in Europe?" "God, I am really going to miss you."

"Jamie, honey, I'm going to miss you too," squealed Victoria, as they rounded a steep curve heading back to Victoria's house. "But you are going to see that I am not going to make it to Europe, the way you are driving." "Did you suck some cocaine up your nose in the loo or something?"

"Oh, Vicky, you are crazy, you know I don't do that crap."

"OOOOOOOOh my dear, you don't know what you are missing," Victoria laughingly responded.

"You know I am worried about you, you won't have me to watch over your crazy little self, and you will probably get hurt in that strange place."

"You are kidding, right?" Victoria, now appearing serious.

"Yeah, I know you can take care of yourself," Jamie giggling "I am jealous, I want to go with you."

"This is exactly why my parents and your grandfather would never allow it." "They know we would drink booze, and chase around with great looking guys, and have wild sex, instead of studying." This sent both girls into a flutter of giggles.

"You know I am more worried about you," stated Victoria sincerely.

"And why would that be?"

"Because that grandmother of yours is nuts, she is a mean old evil woman."

"That is pretty harsh, Vicky."

"Well, she is." "Look how she treats you, and do you know what she told my mom?"

"What?"

"You have to promise not to tell anyone I told you this." "Especially, from who and where you heard it." "You promise?" Victoria prodded with urgency.

Not knowing if she wanted to hear this, Jamie nodded yes.

"She said you weren't really her granddaughter, that you weren't Victor's."

Jamie couldn't respond. The rest of the ride to Victoria's was silent. Reaching the front of the Shelly house, Jamie sat quietly as Victoria collected her belongings to go inside. "Jamie, I'm so sorry I made you cry."

"You didn't."

"Listen, you know that is not true, you look like your father." "She is jealous of you, and everyone knows it." "Even my parents have said that it is disgraceful how she treats you." "Please, I don't want to go off to Europe with you mad at me, I couldn't bear it."

Slowly Jamie turned her face toward Victoria. "Vicky, I am not mad at you, I don't blame you, it just hurts to know she hates me for being her flesh and blood." "As mean as she has been, I wish it wasn't this way, I wish I could love her." With that, they embraced saying goodbye for the summer.

Once again, her room was her refuge. Jamie sat quietly looking out over the fields as the sunset, and reflecting on the day, her conversation with Vicky, and the summer without her close friend. She was so wrapped up in her thoughts, the knock at the door startled her. Chester stood looking at her with worry, a silver dinner tray in his hand. "It was lonely at dinner without you there; I decided since you weren't coming to me, I would come to you." Jamie smiled at his glowing concern and obvious affection for her.

"I can't think of a more handsome and deserving gentleman to have dinner with, in my room." He eagerly entered setting down the dinner entries on the marble bedside table, and placed chairs on either side. When he started to close the glass doors onto the terrace, Jamie protested gently. "Please, can we leave those open?" "I love the sounds of the night, and the air is so fresh."

"Certainly, we can leave them open, whatever my lovely granddaughter wants." Most of the meal was spent eating and listening to the sounds that drifted in through the glass doors. After they finished dinner, Jamie stood to go retrieve a sweater from her closet.

"It is still a bit chilly at night," Jamie said. Chester looked at the fireplace, bare of wood.

"Have you ever used that this year?"

"No, I really have never started a fireplace by myself."

"Well, why didn't you tell me?" "We will fix that right now." Before Jamie could protest, Chester had left the room in a whirl, collected logs in his arms, and a bottle of red wine under his chin, and returned. "Let me show you how to do this." He gave her a lesson in how to stack and light the logs so they would burn efficiently. He then poured two glasses of wine, pulling up pillows for them to set on in front of the fireplace.

"You are going to let me drink alcohol?"

"Only if you are not going to turn me into the sheriff." "One glass and no more." Chester chuckled.

"Well, I wouldn't think of it, but what do you think Sophia will say?"

"Nothing, if she wants to stay alive."

Jamie laughed loudly and sipped the wine, which had a wonderful warm calming effect, chasing away traces of the sadness she had felt.

The evening was an absolute delight. During the evening conversation, Chester asked Jamie what she would most like to do for the summer. Jamie sat with her head down, and softly responded, "I want to go to Gray Mountain, see my old friends, and visit my mother's grave." "Then I want to see aunt Audrey and uncle Ralph in California." "Uncle Ralph hasn't been really healthy for a while." "He had a heart attack and has not been very strong since."

When Jamie raised her head, she found Chester starring deeply into her eyes.

"Jamie, I am so selfish."

"No, you are not."

"Yes honey, I am afraid I am." "This whole time you've been here, I have been enjoying your company so much; I neglected to realize that you left family and friends behind that you love very much." "I am sorry," shaking his head.

"No, no," Jamie exclaimed, "please don't feel bad," she rose to her knees putting her arms around his neck. "You gave me a reason to care again." "After my mother was killed, I felt so helpless and alone, but you showed me life goes on, and what a wonderful life you have given me." "I love you, Grandfather," "oh, I mean......."

"Nah, no, no, Jamie, just call me Grandfather, it sounds good now." "You dear sweet child, pack your bags and plan for your summer trip first to Gray Mountain, and then California." Chester stood pulling Jamie to her feet, hugging her so tight she could hardly breathe, and uttering a tender, "goodnight," then exited the room.

CHAPTER IX

The visit to Gray Mountain was as expected; joyous. Jamie stayed at James Patterson's ranch, just at the edge of Gray Mountain. During the two weeks, she spent in the quaint town there was a constant stream of invitations to parties, brunch, or dinner at old friend's homes. Phone calls as well as gifts were received at the ranch. The only quiet moments were those talking with James and visiting her mother's gravesite.

"How can there be no leads at all?" "I mean, Gray Mountain is a small place, two men just waltz into to town, kill my mother in cold blood, then run out and everyone had a memory loss?" "How is this even possible?" Jamie exclaimed.

"I know it seems bizarre Jamie, I am just as frustrated as you," replied James. The conversation began during what was supposed to be a quiet farewell dinner with James at the ranch. Jamie knew she could not possibly go the entire stay without exploring the subject of her mother's untimely death.

"I know you are James, and you will never know how much I love you for the vigilance you have shown in pursuing my mother's killer." "But I just do not understand, nor can I accept, no leads."

"The only hint of a lead died on death row in Florida."

"What?" .... "What did you say?" asked a visibly shocked Jamie.

"The drifter, the no account, they put to death in Florida." "You know the one who bragged to another inmate about Gray Mountain."

"I am sorry James, I feel like I'm in a bad movie, I do not know what you are talking about!"

"Jamie, I wrote this to you, I called, but you didn't return the calls, I thought you were just trying to forget, I....." James stuttered, dropped his head, nearly in tears.

"Just stop James; first just tell me what happened, as I have never supposedly heard this before."

James responded slowly, softly, "this SOB bragged about how much money he had made in his long sick career as a hit man and mentioned a situation in Gray Mountain that had netted him some money." "Jamie,

I wrote all this to you when I sent the last pictures of the town."

Jamie now angry and confused jumped to her feet. "What letter?" "What pictures?" "Who did you send them to?" "I was never told anything; I did not see any pictures." "God, that old bitch, I just know it was her!"

"Jamie, honey who are you talking about?" "That so-called grandmother of mine." "No one, except her and my father, would dare do anything like this, and he is too drunk most of the time." Both sat in silence, trying with difficulty, to mull over the dreadful truth.

"OK, just.... please tell me now, who was this guy?"

"Well, last fall the sheriff received a call from some authorities in Florida." "They claimed there was a guy on death row that had been bragging to anyone who would listen about how many people he had been paid to kill." "Saying how he had never been caught, in twenty years of killing, and wouldn't have been if an intended victim hadn't shot him in the thigh with a gun at his last job." "His name was Robert Sawyer, and he had mentioned a job in Gray Mountain he had been hired to do." "Ed Swanson and I flew down to Tampa." "We tried to get the authorities to let us talk to him, and we did see him." "But he had grown irrational and confused." "He just talked gibberish." "No family or friends, no residence, just a box full of junk that meant nothing, and this idiot." "They then put him to death a week later." "It has been so disappointing," shaking his head, "I wanted to bring to justice the scum that destroyed the most beautiful woman I have ever known." "I have failed in doing that."

Jamie stood staring at this broken man. He had aged dreadfully since she last saw him; tears were streaming down his face. She knew the main reason for this, was her mother's death, and his inability to do anything about it. Her rage and anger were replaced with pity for this man who loved her mother and wanted justice as much as she. She walked to him sitting down on his lap, and softly kissing his forehead, "James, my mother would not like to see you defeated." "She would tell you to get up and get to work."

Right up until Jamie boarded the plane for California, she never saw James without tears in his eyes. It broke her heart, but in a twisted way alleviated some of her own grief replacing it with a hate so deep and piercing, it left her physically shaken when dwelling on the events she had learned about.

CHAPTER X

The sunsets over the Pacific were just as she remembered; spectacular. Every sunrise, every sunset, rain or shine Jamie was at her favorite spot on the beach relishing in the panorama before her. It comforted her, seeming to remind her life would go on and much of it is magnificent.

She noticed the figure walking toward her far down the beach, even before she sat down on her favorite flattop rock, close to the windswept waves of the ocean. It irritated her, this was her time with nature and even though the figure moved slowly, stopping every now and then on its journey toward her, she could not fully concentrate on her solitude. She would close her eyes, hearing only the sound of the waves and the song of the gulls. As the sun rose higher in the sky the waves seemed to rise up to meet daylight; ......and that confounded figure moved closer. She began to make out another figure, that of a dog running happily into the ocean's waves to retrieve something the figure was throwing. The figure was male, and as he approached it became apparent he was not only young but noticeably attractive. His hair was just a bit too long, thick, curly, and black. It was obvious he was enjoying the game he was playing with his dog, a large blonde Labrador retriever. As he passed Jamie he looked at her, he nodded and smiled. Jamie returned the gesture. At that moment, he threw the Frisbee again in the air toward the incoming waves. The wind caught it sending it hurling back toward Jamie. Without giving the action a thought, Jamie jumped to her feet and caught the Frisbee effortlessly. The dog ran to her feet looking up at her standing on the rock, he whined as if to say, "please give it back." Jamie looked down into his huge watery brown eyes and began to laugh. He appeared pitiful but amusing. She handed back the Frisbee to the dog. His owner appeared behind him.

He reached out his hand, and said: "I thank you, and so does Bud here." Jamie smiled back and shivered a bit. He held her hand longer than what would have been expected as he waited for a response. Jamie's response was slow to come because she was studying him. He was gorgeous. His hair tousled about his head, eyes very dark brown, his features looked Hispanic with almost an aristocratic air, and he spoke with a definite British accent.

"I am glad I could be of assistance to Bud, and you of course," Bud whined again, and they both laughed. He was still holding her hand; they were staring into one another's eyes, as he bent over and kissed her on the lips. She responded, and it was sweet, yet seemed somewhat thrilling. This continued for three more kisses until suddenly she awoke from this dream. They both seemed to come back to reality at the same time.

Again, they stood staring, mesmerized. He spoke first, "Th....that is the first time I've ever done anything like that." "Are you a witch or a temptress or something?"

"I was thinking the same thing about you," Jamie responded in a soft monotone voice.

"Well, I am feeling sort of foolish here," Bud whined again, continuing to look up at Jamie with his head cocked to one side. "I think Bud is feeling the same as I am." "If you would consider allowing me to make up for taking advantage of your good nature, by taking you to breakfast?" "Maybe we could talk about this over tea." "What do you say?"

Jamie stood silent.

"There is a little café right around the cove up here, and I know the owner." "Have I made you frightened of me?" "I really am sorry for my behavior, and I promise not to touch you, that is unless......."

Jamie reached out and again took his hand which silenced him, "I am not afraid, I am just shocked at my own behavior." "I think breakfast is a wonderful idea." "Shall we just walk?"

"I would like that." He responded.

They walked in silence for a bit, with Jamie being the first to break it. "I have been coming to the beach every morning for nearly two weeks, and this is the first time I have seen you and Bud on this stretch of beach."

Smiling, he replied, "that is because this is the first time in a while I have been back to this beach." "Nearly a year ago I bought a small place about two miles round the bend back there, on Gull Beach." "Are you familiar with it?"

"Yes, I am." "My uncle Ralph owns a deep-sea fishing and tour business, and he mentioned Gull Beach before when we were out on the boat."

"Your uncle, his name isn't Ralph Keck by chance?"

"Why yes, you know him, and my aunt Audrey?"

"I'm afraid so."

"What do you mean you're afraid?"

"No, no, nothing like that, I mean, they may not be all that pleased with me for boldly kissing you, without being properly introduced."

Giggling openly, Jamie responded, "well then maybe we should start with a name." "I know Bud's here, but yours is..?"

"Alex, my name is Alex; Alex Buchanan."

"I am very pleased to meet you Alex." "And mine is Jamie Blackstone." "There, now they can't say we weren't properly introduced, even though in retrospect." They both laughed aloud, as they entered the back door of the Shipwreck Inn.

The majority of her time in California was spent with Alex. He was an absolute delight; funny, lighthearted, and deliciously attractive. She learned

Alex was a college graduate from UCLA. His major was in Journalism, and at present a freelance writer; in addition, a helicopter pilot for the Coast Guard. His family lived in the Dominican Republic. Alex chose to stay in California after college because of job ties, and close friendships. He was completely and totally without attachment, and he liked it. He was easy to talk to, not knowing a great deal about this young man, never had it ever been so easy to trust someone she knew so little about. She shared everything with him, her innermost thoughts and feelings, the story of her mother's death, her relationship with the various family members, and of course, Ronnie.

They took romantic moonlight walks on the beach nearly every night. He took her to casual parties introducing her to his friends. He read to her, held her, made love to her, and most of all made her feel like life was safe and adventurous, filled with beauty.

When it was time to return to Richmond, Virginia, they pledged undying love and friendship, promising to always keep in touch, never to let the bond break knowing what they had was good, but perhaps not a bond that would carry them into the distant future together.

"Going back to Ronnie, now are we?"

"Alex, you are really exasperating at times, you know that don't you?"

"Yes, that is part of my charm, don't you think?"

"Well, I have one thing up on that old Ronnie."

"Oh yea, what would that be?"

"I had you first!" Picking her up off her feet, swinging her around until she was dizzy, and then tossing her into an ocean wave.

"Damn you, Alex, I did not want to get wet today," as she clumsily stood back up in the slushy sand. "I am supposed to be at the airport in six hours."

"Well, maybe it is just my unconscious desire to keep you here, and to ravage your beautiful body on a daily basis." They both began to laugh, she running after him down the beach. He came to a halt, and she abruptly bumped into him. "Jamie, you know I just had a thought." "Why am I letting you fly on a commercial airline when I have a friend who has a fleet of air ambulances?" "He might consent to us flying you home with my assistance of course." "Surely your grandfather would rather have a pair of able-bodied young champions flying you instead of a dull, lonely, and possibly dangerous commercial flight." "What do you say?"

"I say that would be wonderful except for one thing."

"And what might that be?"

"My grandfather would never put me on a commercial flight silly." "I am going to the airport, but to a private airstrip located behind the main airport where my grandfather will pick me up in his plane." "I really could not disappoint him at this late date." "I am sure he will be excited to see me, I know I am him." "You do understand, don't you?"

"No, I am mad as hell," he stated turning his back on Jamie.

"Alex, do you mean it?" With that, he turned again picking her up and squeezing the breath from her body.

"Do I look mad?" Smiling in a huge white tooth exaggerated way.

"God, you are awful."

"Am I?" He suddenly took on a more serious tone teasingly rubbing her nipple with his thumb. He looked deep into her eyes, kissing her so tenderly, slipping his hands beneath her sheer top and caressing her breasts. Looking around at a deserted beach he gently lifted her top and began kissing then sucking her nipples and massaging between her thighs. Her head dropped back as a low moan escaped from her mouth. His hands slid behind on her lower back under her clothing, down her buttocks, squeezing her, pushing her against him. The sheer skirt fell to her ankles, she jerked back to look down both sides of the beach.

"There is no one baby; we will be able to see them come from a mile or more away."

"Yeah," she playfully bit his lower lip, "and who do you think is going to be watching for them, huh?" He pulled down her panties diving into her nest of hair, driving his tongue into her, sucking and licking until she fell back on to the sand. He attacked her again with the same maneuver until she cried out as the waves pulled the sand beneath their bodies. He now pushed his hard expanse into her, rhythmically moving slowly at first continuing to kiss and suck on her mouth and breasts. The sounds of the ocean, the waves' attempt to pull them in, and the sea mist only added to this intoxicating encounter. The climax seemed to go on and on for both of them. It was the most incredible sex Jamie had ever experienced. Had the entire city decided to walk up on the beach that day, they could not have stopped. When the act was complete, with a return to reality they both sat up looking around. The beach still deserted.

"My God Alex."

"SHHHH, Jamie please just don't say anything," placing a finger over her lips. "Let us let it end here, with this most perfect moment."

"But I do not want it to end forever, just for today," Jamie said with great earnest.

"Yes, my darling, but for today, let's leave it at perfect." "You know how to reach me if you need anything." He leaned to kiss her one brief final time, "I love you." He stood, looking down at her and smiling.

"I love you too," she responded. He waved slightly and then walked toward his residence down the beach.

CHAPTER XI

Summer had been an exasperating roller coaster of emotion; sadness, and frustration, and then elation, and tenderness of feeling. Jamie was leaving California reluctantly. She loved it here. She worried about Audrey and Ralph. Uncle Ralph did not look healthy. He could not walk fast or climb even two steps without having chest pain. Aunt Audrey shared with Jamie news that made her worry even more. "We have been to see one of the best cardiologists in the country," lamented Audrey. "They said he is inoperable for bypass surgery." "There is a procedure they call TMR, and they make these tiny holes in the muscle of the heart, and it is supposed to build a larger blood supply and reduce the chest pain he has all the time."

"So why hasn't he had this done, Aunt Audrey?"

"Because he said he just isn't ready to have his chest sawed open." "You know men, they are stubborn, especially this man." "I just hope I don't find him dead someday."

"God Audrey, that is awful to even think about."

"Yeah, it really is, but Jamie there is something I need to talk to you about." "If anything were to happen to Ralph, I would never stay here by myself." "I would move closer to L.A. where I have some friends." "It would just be too lonely here."

"Aunt Audrey, why are you even talking like this?"

"Jamie, I have thought about this often." "You know our property here on this beach is worth a good deal of money." "Ralph has all but sold out the remainder of his fishing and guide business to Gordon Murphy, and that is worth even more." "I really have more money then I will ever need." "As I'm sure you do, or will as well, considering you are an heir to the Blackstone fortune." "What I am trying to say is, I really do not want to sell this house on the beach, I just do not want to live here full time alone." "Would you be interested in being part owner with me?" "You would always have this place to come to, and...." Jamie was already crying, as she wrapped her arms around Audrey's neck.

"Of course, I would, I have always loved this beach house, well, it is part of the family, don't you think?"

The remainder of the walk they had taken by the ocean was in silence, both crying, holding tight to one another's hand.

The reunion with her grandfather was not what she had hoped for. The jet was there, he wasn't. The same crew that originally flew her from Gray Mtn. to Virginia was present. "Where is my grandfather?"

"He was called away on emergency business Miss Blackstone," the co-pilot said.

"Is everyone all right?"

"As far as I know."

"Will someone be picking me up?"

"I'm sure they will Miss."

So much for this conversation, thought Jamie. The trip was so quiet, she fell asleep in route, and not even the landing aroused her. Not until a complete stop and the attendant tapped her shoulder, did Jamie become aware they had completed the trip and landed at the Richmond airstrip.

As she walked off the plane she saw Charles standing by the gray limo. "Welcome back home Miss Jamie, we all shor have missed your pretty face." He reached out and hugged Jamie, much to the flight crew's amazement.

"Charles, I have missed you too."

"Is everyone else, all right?" "I believe so Miss Jamie." "Your granddaddy was real sorry he couldn't make it." "He shor was disappointed, somethin about a hostile takeover of some a his stock." "He was real angry when he took on outa here this mornin." "He gave me strict instructions to explain everythin to you."

"You did good Charles, I feel better since you have explained it all to me." "Tell me about everyone else."

"Well, all us common folk haven't changed much." "Time jus rolls by us without alota clatter." Jamie smiled at his frankness about life.

"Your grandmother has been real testy lately.... she just ain't happy a tall." "I suspect because your father has been leavin at night a lot, and not a comin back till the next day or two." "He starts his drinkin in the mornin and doesn't stop until he's just stewed." "Every day." Jamie sat quietly as Charles continued on. "Even if he does try to sneak into the kitchen and grab a bite to eat, she is a bitchin at him, and he just can't take it, he just can't." Charles was shaking his head obviously distressed by the depressing situation he continued to describe. "I'm worried about your daddy." "He is a gettin thin, and that old boozin can't be good for his liver."

"Where has my grandfather been through all of this?"

"Well honey, he been spending alota time away from the ranch, jus like his son."

"Where has Ronnie been?" "He has been around, workin as usual." "When he ain't workin, he's gone too." "It's a sad place at the ranch, a sad place." "But our light just returned with you, Miss Jamie." "We all so glad your back." "We shor did miss ya." "We shor enough did." "I been wantin to tell you Miss Jamie, I am worried about you."

"Why Charles, why about me?"

"Well that grandmother of yours just seems to be full a so much hate, an I don know why." "I know some of it cause you're there, and everyone jus loves you, Miss Jamie." "It jus seems like the more you're loved, the more hateful she is." "The more hateful she is, the more she's a driven everyone way," "I tell ya, she jus the loneliest most hateful old women I ever seen."

The remainder of the trip was quiet, and Jamie was in deep thought. The ride into the ranch was as beautiful as she remembered. The horses made her anxious to see Redman.

"How is my horse?"

"Jus like you, pretty as ever." "He will be glad to see you." "Ronnie has been exercising him."

"Ronnie has been riding my horse?" Jamie said with awe.

"Na, I don't think he's been a ridin him, jus runnin him at the end of a rope." "He's been a groomin him though, keepin him beautiful." Jamie was smiling, beginning to feel a familiar tingling sensation. "Well, here we are," Charles leaned up over the seat before stepping out to open the door for Jamie. "You be careful now, ya hear?" "I'll be close by if you need me, all right?"

"All right Charles," a bit startled at his obvious concern for her. Jamie hurried to her room. Her first action was to call Victoria, learning she would return from Europe the end of the week. Jamie changed her clothes to more casual wear and ran down the long stairway to the kitchen, where servants were waiting to greet her. She learned that none of the Blackstone family was expected home for dinner. Jamie announced they would have their own private party in the kitchen. Some of the servants protested, afraid of Sophia's response if they were caught socializing with a Blackstone. But Jamie insisted so all agreed they would participate.

Next, she would go to the barns to see Redman and Ronnie. When she called him, Redman greeted her with his usual show of speed and a bit of prancing; she spent time scratching behind his ears, which he responded to with head shaking, and lip extensions. Ronnie was nowhere in sight. She walked into the barn, and nothing. She finally proceeded to the tack room. It was full of saddles and blankets, bridles, hackamores, and ropes; it smelled of rich leather and polish. At the back of the tack room was a doorway which led to Ronnie's living quarters.

The door was ajar, and she stepped in, "Ronnie, are you here?" No answer to her question. She walked in farther to his kitchen. It was definitely masculine.

All the cabinets, bookcases, tables, and woodwork were covered with pine, burnished a reddish tan. The connecting room had wine colored leather furnishings covered with beautiful Indian motif blankets and pillows. The floors of mosaic inlet tiles and braided rugs lay in various locations. Walls in a white adobe-like finish, the only modern appearing furnishing was a huge entertainment unit taking up one entire wall.

She loved it; the whole place felt like it should set near a desert spa; his warm fuzzy space. She began looking at pictures on the bookcase, of his family.

"Looking for something?" She nearly jumped into the bookcase, turning quickly to see him standing behind her.

"Ah, no, no, certainly not, actually I was looking for you." "And, I was so enthralled by your decor; I sort of made myself at home." "I'm sorry."

He grinned, "So what do you think?" "A little rough for you I suspect."

"Actually not, it feels good, comfortable, cozy, like I could curl up on that big couch, among all those pillows, and take a nap."

"Well?"

"Well, what?"

"Well, why don't you?" She felt her heart jump, and the tingling started.

"Umm, actually I slept on the plane, and I'm not tired." "But I would just sit down and talk to you a bit."

He walked closer to her, and bent even closer, she could feel his breath on her face; the fire had started. "You see, I am a working man, and I can't just sit and chat whenever I feel the need, I don't have a whole summer to vacation like some do." The tone was sarcastic, soft, and sexy.

With her face glowing red, eyes cast downward, "I see, well I suppose I should get out of your way so you can work." "Thank you for caring for Redman this summer, he looks wonderful."

"Yeah, he is a horse on this ranch, and that is what I do." Jamie was close to tears. She wasn't sure what message he was sending, but it was hurting. She started for the door when he grabbed her arm. She looked into his eyes, "I don't work all night you know." "You ah, wanta come back later?" "We can talk then." "How about eight?"

Jamie took a deep breath, "I'll be here," turning and walking slowly out the door.

"Fuck, I can't believe I just did that," throwing his hat to the ground.

Jamie walked just outside the barn, then ran all the way to the house, smiling.

The dinner with the servants, ranch hands, and Charles went off well. She told them all the news of her summer vacation, leaving out the news about her mother, and rendezvous with Alex. Laughter filled the kitchen galley once again. However, the entire time Jamie was nervous. She couldn't wait for it to end. At 7:30 she excused herself with the explanation she was very tired and was retiring early.

Once in her room, she freshened for her encounter with Ronnie. She locked her bedroom door behind her, in case her grandfather came home and had a need to check on her. She knew he would assume she was sleeping and not attempt to enter. One of the maids had previously shown her a back stairway leading to a storage area off the kitchen galley. She would use that way to enter and exit. She did so easily, and through the darkness made her way to the barn. Jamie knocked on his door, but no answer. "Please tell me he didn't do this to me." She knocked again, and then turned the knob, "Ronnie?"

"Yeah, come on in," she was relieved. He was sitting on the couch watching a football game on television. He was in a pair of jeans as usual, with no shirt. He looked incredible.

"You want a beer?"

"No, I don't want to contribute to you going to jail."

"Why not, I probably will anyway."

"What makes you say that?"

"I don't know," he responded again with a sarcastic tone.

"Look I didn't come here for you to talk to me like I am dirt on your boots."

"Just what did you come here for?" He was on his feet ready for confrontation. "What could I possibly have that someone like you would want?" "My big pillows and blankets?" "Here take them." He threw a pillow and blanket at her.

Now Jamie was angry, hurt, and yelling as well, "I really don't know why I am here." "Because I am stupid enough to believe there is something between us." "I wanted to find out what that something is, but you can just go to hell, you sonofabitch." She was running for the door when he caught her and whirled her around, so they were nose to nose, "My mother is not a bitch."

She put her hand on his face, "I know." He kissed her again and again. They were both so hungry for this moment neither could let go. They staggered to the couch and continued kissing. Jamie made the first move by unzipping his pants and exposing him. She bent to take him into her mouth. He moaned and arched backward. She slid down between his legs, and he grabbed her by the shoulders, hauling her up onto his lap.

"Jamie please," he whispered.

"I am trying baby." She clutched his hard penis in her hand and began to massage. He let out a howl, throwing her back against the couch.

"God damn it, Jamie, stop it."

"Why, what is wrong with you?"

"What is wrong with you, girl?" "Why can't you see?"

"See what?" "Why do we always end up like this?" He grabbed her again pulling her up on her feet.

Through clenched teeth, he said, "You are Chester's seventeen-year-old granddaughter." "I am a ranch hand with a hell of a lot of respect and gratitude for that man, and here I am about to fuck her." "Jesus Jamie, can't you see I am about to explode?" "I want you so bad, I could sweat blood." "But this isn't the way." Jamie stood attempting to bring herself from a disheveled state. Ronnie stood leaning against the wall, head down.

She placed a hand on his shoulder, "as long as we are speaking the truth here, let me inform you of a couple of things." "My grandfather loves you like a son, he doesn't just respect you, he loves you, more than his own son." "You would have to be blind not to see that, everyone else does, including Sophia." Ronnie looked up at Jamie, stone-faced. "The other thing is, I love you too." "Every part of my body aches to be near you." "I might be seventeen, but I know the difference between sex and love." "You call me when you figure it out." Jamie walked out the door, up the hill to the house and into her room.

CHAPTER XII

The next morning Chester was waiting for Jamie to come down to breakfast. He had even sent the maid to inquire when that might be. When Jamie entered the dining area, Chester was standing next to the table smiling. He hurriedly went to her hugging her. "Boy have I missed you."

"I missed you too Chester."

"Chester!" "What happened to grandfather?" Jamie laughed at him. "Well, let us have some breakfast, and you can tell me all about your trip to Montana, and California." "By the way, I am sorry I wasn't there to greet you." "It was a little business problem."

"Yes, I know Charles told me."

"Well isn't this a cozy little brunch for two." Victor quipped sarcastically

"It could be for three," Jamie responded sweetly, which took both Victor and Chester by surprise.

"Well you know I might, I am a bit hungry this fine morn." Victor sat by his daughter and tried to muster a smile. "So how was your trip to California?"

"Wonderful, beautiful, yet sad."

132

"Odd combination, why sad?"

"I guess because of Uncle Ralph's health." "He has a very bad heart you know." "He can't walk far without having chest pain, so he was forced to sell his business and some of his beach land holdings." "It has made him depressed; he really didn't talk much, just stared at the ocean." "The whole thing is very hard on Aunt Audrey."

"I am sorry to hear that Jamie." "Ralph and Audrey are fine people." "I liked the time I spent with them, and I guess always regretted just leaving, and never talking with them again, especially Ralph." "They were never anything but kind to me, never judgmental." Victor was shaking his head slowly back and forth with his eyes closed. Chester and Jamie sat quietly watching him. Jamie wasn't sure if she was more amazed by the emotion she heard in his voice or the obvious anguish present on his face.

"You could go and see them, you know." "I would go with you," Jamie said hopefully. Victor remained quiet, eyes closed, forehead resting in his hands.

Chester broke the silence with an additional revelation, "it would not hurt us all to go." "These people are Jamie's only family left from her mother's side of the family." "I believe it would have pleased her mother to know that we are attempting to be charitable." "A feeble attempt at making up for the shabby way we treated you and your mother, when you were born." Jamie could not speak, for the large lump that grew in her throat. Her eyes filled with tears, spilling onto her cheeks. Victor opened his eyes, looking first at Chester, then his daughter.

He reached out for Jamie, hugging her tightly to him, smiling he exclaimed, "So when do we leave?" There was a nervous laughter from the three, like the warmth and closeness they were feeling was too foreign to completely deal with.

The warmth dissipated quickly as Sophia entered the room. "Victor, I have been looking for you." "I thought we were going into Richmond for brunch." "Why are you here at this table eating?" Sophia's voice resembled fingernails on a blackboard.

"Sophia, shut-up," Chester responded with disgust.

"You know I really am growing very sick and tired of the way I am being treated by all of you, in my own house!" Sophia's voice was elevating higher and louder with each word." "I do not have to tolerate this behavior from any of you," she screeched. "Ever since we allowed this little.... into our home, you have both shown me nothing but disrespect!"

Chester was now on his feet, "you will not speak of my granddaughter in that manner." His face was crimson, his voice shaking, "I cannot remember the last time I had any respect for you." Victor rose, gently pushing Chester down in his chair.

Looking steadily at Sophia, Victor said in slow deliberate words, "I am going to Richmond by myself, not for brunch, but to get drunk again." "I stay drunk mother, so I will be numb enough not to feel the pain."

"Victor, Sophia pleaded, let me go with you, we will have a nice lunch, we'll shop, go to the races and forget all this nastiness." Victor stepped closer to Sophia; she had never seen this kind of loathing coming from her son.

"You just don't get it do you?" Victor hissed. "I hate you for what you have done to me, and this family." "I stay drunk just to tolerate living." "Every time I close my eyes I see Mary." "Beautiful, beautiful

Mary." His voice cracked, and he began to cry, "I loved her, I was so selfish and weak."

"Victor," Sophia shouted. She reached out for his arm and he threw her off, glaring at her with such hatred it frightened her. He ran from the room. Jamie was sobbing, as Chester sat attempting to console her. Sophia walked unsteadily to her room as the servants peered around the corner being the audience to all the commotion in the dining area.

Chester sat quietly beside Jamie, rubbing her back and shoulders allowing her to stop crying, and relax her body. "I am so sorry, honey."

For the remainder of the day, the statuesque mansion seemed empty of life. Bodies were scattered in the wake of destruction left from the morning family confrontation.

Victor made good on his word; he had retreated to Richmond, diving into the first bottle of bourbon available, accompanied then by willing female companionship. Like father like son, after calming Jamie, seeing her to her room, where she withdrew into a fitful sleep and where she remained, Chester fled to the arms of Erma Maples.

Sophia stayed in her room as well. She refused to come out to eat, or even to partake of her afternoon tea, which in previous times was a must. She sulked, sobbed, paced, and stared into her vanity mirror like the witch in Snow White, talking to her image. "How could Victor have said those things to me?" "I have given him all of me." "Everything I have ever done has been for him." "It is because of her, that demon spawn." "A product of that red-headed whore." "Because of some misguided knowledge he believes she is his child, but I know different." "He is once again poisoned by her presence, so you leave me no alternative, Victor." "I will not have my life, nor yours ruined by this cloud of evil she has brought into our house." "Oh God, will we ever be rid of this curse?" Putting her face in her hands, and quietly crying.

When Jamie awoke, it was with a jolt. Her heart was beating very fast, and she was sweating. She could hear bells ringing. It was the telephone, why wasn't anyone answering it? She reached for the receiver near her bed. "Yes, this is Jamie."

"Jamie, this is Nora in the kitchen." "Honey, would you like me to bring you up a dinner tray?"

Jamie, still somewhat groggy, remained silent. "Jamie dear, are you, all right?"

"Yes Nora, I'm all right, I guess I'm still kind of sleepy." "You don't need to bring me a tray." "I need to get out of this room anyway." "Is anyone else down there from the family?"

"Just us help," Nora replied.

"I'm not very hungry Nora, my stomach is upset."

"I know just the thing to perk you up." "I will fix you a small bowl of my special perk me up homemade chicken noodle soup, with a slice of bread Marie made this morning, and a glass of cold milk, all good for what ails ya." Jamie smiled at her concern and mothering.

"That sounds good Nora; I'll be down in about 30."

Jamie felt empty and very cold. So much so she was shaking; feeling chilled she showered letting the hot water run on her until she finally felt warm. The dryer for her hair felt even better. She continued to blow her hair long after it was dry. Pulling on fleece pants and shirt, she finally made her way to the kitchen where Nora waited patiently. The fire was going in the hearth, so she sat quietly in front of it eating the delicious warm soup and listening to the evening news as Nora and Marie cleaned the kitchen. "Where is everyone?" "Isn't anyone else eating tonight?"

"There isn't anyone here, honey." "No one returned from town." "We thought maybe they had decided to eat in Richmond," knowing in her heart that was not true. Nora and Marie had overheard the shouting in the dining area that morning. They had discussed the happenings with Charles and Ronnie. Everyone knew sooner or later Sophia would return. However, it was doubtful they would see Victor or Chester until the next day. They all felt Jamie had been abandoned by those who would protect her from Sophia, so they would assume the role.

As Jamie stared into the fire, the back door opened and Charles walked in, followed by Ronnie. Jamie looked down, and then back into the glow of the fire. Charles walked to Jamie's side, lightly rubbing her back. "How's my pretty little friend this fine evenin?" His voice was so soft, it was almost a whisper. The tenderness made Jamie's eyes well up with tears.

Charles bent down, putting his arms around her shoulders, "if I could take this pain away for you, and take it to myself, you know I would." Jamie buried her face on his sleeve, tears continuing to come. The rest stood silently, now James the butler had joined them.

Ronnie wanted to walk to her and comfort her. She looked so young, so soft and beautiful. God how his heart ached to hold her, love her. The audible sound was rain beating against the window pane, and the logs crackling in the fire.

"You know on a chilly rainy evening like this, I propose we all have a fine rollicking game of cribbage." James the butler interjected shattering the uncomfortable silence for which Jamie was grateful.

"Well, I don know about no cribbage, but I do know how to play some poker," replied Charles. This brought a chuckle from everyone.

"So, poker it is," laughed Nora. For the next two hours, the six of them sat in a circle at the table near the hearth, playing poker, laughing, enjoying the warmth of one another's company and thanking God for every minute Sophia had not returned.

After the game had finished, they continued to just sit and converse about anything that came to mind. Jamie was enjoying herself immensely. Especially since Ronnie was near, and through the entire evening the invisible electric current between them was apparent, particularly when their eyes met. By 10pm everyone knew Sophia was not returning either. The decision was made to have a brandy as a nightcap, then retire for the evening. A toast was made by James, as Jamie held her glass of milk up, "a bit of cliché, but here is to friendship, peace, and love," clinking glasses, followed by liquid warmth.

Jamie hugged everyone before leaving the kitchen for her bedroom. "You are all my friends, even more, part of my family." "You are so good to me, thank you."

Ronnie walked Jamie to the foot of the stairs, then up the stairs to her room. "Are you feeling like you will sleep?"

"No, I slept all afternoon, so I will probably watch some television." He stood silent, looking down at the floor. "Would you consider coming in and watching with me?" "Or are you afraid I might lead you astray again?"

Ronnie looked deeply into her eyes, and her stomach felt like it turned inside out. He was silent for what seemed to Jamie like an uncomfortable amount of time, in reality, it was only seconds. "Maybe what I am more afraid of is that you won't." She was breathless.

He cupped her face in his hands kissing her gently on the lips. Now she was warm. He opened her door; reaching for her he picked her up off her feet and carried her into her bedroom, kicking the door shut behind him. They stood in the darkness kissing over and over, both desiring to move slowly, knowing they were about to approach ecstasy; a moment they both had dreamt of.

He pulled off her sweatshirt, she had not bothered to put on a bra, so her breasts were susceptible to his touch, so very soft, yet nipples rock hard. She unbuttoned his shirt, and he assisted her. He pulled her to him, he was so warm; he massaged her breasts, reached down in her panties as she moaned and whispered his name. He reached over pulling back the bed linens and removed the rest of his and her clothing. He laid her back on the bed, spreading her. She pulled him closer to her, rolling on top of him. He was determined to wait, he did not want to have release at this time, "come here sweetheart," lifted her up and placed her beneath him. "I have been saving this for you," he whispered. With that, he pushed himself inside her. She arched back, groaning in absolute rapture. He had never known such a feeling. No one before had felt like her; as sweet, and desirable. He took his time, even though difficult to restrain himself he wanted to relish this moment as long as possible. By the time his pinnacle came, Jamie was overcome with the joy of his love. She cried out in utter elation.

"Oh my God, Ronnie I do love you so much." "I have never felt anything like that." "I don't care what you ever think of me, I know I love you."

"My darling Jamie, I feel exactly the same." He kissed her again and again. He could not get enough of her, nor she of him. They made love two more times before dawn.

When Jamie opened her eyes, Ronnie was gone. He had been gone since the first hint of light. He felt invigorated and was anxious to start the day's chores. All the while he thought about how he was going to tell Chester of his love for his granddaughter. He would provide a good life for her somehow, he would convince Chester the most important thing was their fervent love for one another.

Jamie lay in bed relishing in the aftermath of their love making. She could smell him on her bed sheets. It really was not a dream; it was the most incredible night of her life, and she knew now she could survive anything as long as Ronnie was near. She wondered if her parents had loved this deeply, with such intensity. If they had she could not fathom what her father must be feeling now and had endured after Mary's death. She was more determined than ever to win back his love.

CHAPTER XIII

Charles had returned to his cabin, but too early to retire. He sat on his porch enjoying the sound of the rain, and the taste of bourbon. The sound of the rain drops hitting the roof would comfort him tonight as he slumbered, and he smiled at the thought. He closed his eyes and thought of the cabin he grew up in as a young boy. He remembered on rainy evenings he would snuggle in his warm bed listening to his mother moving about in the kitchen of their modest abode. He could smell the aroma of bread baking, mixed with the odor of burning tobacco coming from his father's corncob pipe. Charles father would be sitting at the kitchen table reading, as his mother baked. There would be delicious warm bread with honey for breakfast, and Charles knew he must find sleep quickly, or his stomach would begin to growl.

Charles was one of seven children. His father was a farm hand, a hardworking man who had ideals that he did not stray from. They were religious people, religious in faith as well as in their everyday dealings with friends, employers and their children. His mother cared for the family, taught the children, cooked, cleaned and baked for many ladies in the town of Richmond. Charles could not remember many bad times when growing up. They could not afford to go to school in the beginning, to purchase clothes and food was difficult enough.

Eventually a small grade school for black children was started in an abandoned barn down the road from where they lived. So, Charles, his brothers, and sister, would travel the road to school every morning during the winter months, to learn to read.

Charles had good memories of growing up on his family's small farm. To this day he missed his parents, who had passed away years before. He didn't know where even one of his brothers were. They all had drifted from the Richmond area. Charles couldn't understand why no one had kept in touch; it was too bad, shaking his head at the thought. His sister Talisa was dead. She died just before her eightieth birthday. Always sickly, it seemed like Talisa caught every flu bug or cold. It was hard for her and seemed to grow worse with each infectious assault. The last time the process migrated into pneumonia, and the final fight was not strong enough to save her. Her death was hard on Charles mother, she never seemed the same.

There was that sound again, ... what was that sound? He strained to hear. It......It.. sounded like snapping, snapping of wood, and twigs as someone would step on them. He stood up and walked to the edge of the porch and peered out into the woods. It was hard to see anything with the rain and the fog; he ducked his head and squinted trying to envision what could be making the noise.

As Charles noticed a movement to his right, he turned. The figure was covered with a black rain coat the hood obliterated the sight of the face. The first blow to the side of his head hurt bad. Charles fell to the porch floor, looked up in disbelief, reaching up toward the figure as he lay there. "Why you doin this?" "Who are........" with the next blow the pain was not as apparent, and from that point on Charles could feel himself being beaten everywhere on his body; he felt and heard his bones break. He wondered why he did not feel any pain, and then knew... he would see his parents this night.

Charles was missed early in the morning. Nora noticed that Charles had not stopped for his usual breakfast coffee before chores. James noticed that the mail and newspaper were not brought in from the front gate. Ronnie noticed that fresh hay bales had not been delivered to the barns and went to the main house to inquire.

When Charles did not show for lunch Nora encouraged Ronnie to go to Charles cabin to check on him. Ronnie believed he might find him hung over, knowing occasionally that had happened, he thought how he would tease him. But, Charles had never not shown up at all. He could possibly be sick, and unable to drive his cart. Maybe he'd had a stroke, and Ronnie would find him unable to move. He shuttered at the thought, and a menacing feeling began to creep over him.

As Ronnie pulled up to the front of the cabin, he could not believe what he was looking at. He slowly exited the truck and walked toward the body that lay in a pool of coagulated blood on the porch. It was obvious Charles had been dead a few hours. His face was swollen and so contorted that if Ronnie had not known who Charles was, with the clothes he was wearing from the night before, he would not have recognized him. His head was smashed open in the back, with a large amount of brain tissue herniating out of his skull.

Someone had entered his cabin, tearing the front door completely off, turning over furniture, pulling drawers out and scattering papers around the floor. Ronnie sat on the front porch swing and wept. He was angry and so nauseated he was sure he would vomit. Why would anyone hurt this sweet gentle man? What could he have that someone would be willing to take his life for?

For a moment, Sophia flashed through his head, he shook off the thought. He knew he must call the authorities and disturb nothing at the scene. He must contact Chester, and Oh God, Jamie.

CHAPTER XIV

Sunset was always such a peaceful time on the ranch. The burnished yellow-red colors were brilliant behind a silhouette of ever-darkening hills and trees. As the sun lost its battle with the blackness of night, twinkling stars made their appearance. The only sounds were faraway contributions to the evening, the faint sound of an airplane engine, on its journey, crickets starting their night symphony. When one sat quietly enjoying the pleasantness of this serenity, it seemed that there could not really be anything bad in the world. No cruelty, or meanness, just beauty.

Jamie smiled sardonically to herself, "what a joke, nothing mean or cruel." "That is all there is." Sitting at the foot of Charles grave site, staring down at the freshly turned earth. All she could feel was anger, with an aching in her heart; a feeling she knew well. But this time the anger was different. It came with a determination to seek out the source of this cowardly deed, not a feeling of helplessness like after her mother was murdered. Sophia was behind this and she would see her punished, she would find the truth about why both these people she loved were swept away from her. She would kill who was responsible.

"Jamie, what are you doing out here?" She didn't even flinch at the sudden appearance of another person in her peaceful misery. Ronnie's voice was gentle, yet firm. "You know you shouldn't be out here alone." "We still don't know what happened, or who made it on to the ranch to hurt Charles, they could still be around."

"Oh no, they are gone, they have been paid you see."

"What are you talking about?"

"I mean whomever she hired was paid, so now they are gone forever."

"She who?"

"Sophia, that's who, the same person who had my mother killed."

"Jamie, for God's sake, Sophia is not capable of killing Charles."

Jamie jumped to her feet. "Stop being stupid!" "You know she hired some thug to do this, to punish me; part of her plan to get rid of me." "Don't you see this?"

"Jamie you need to stop."

"I do not need to stop anything." "In fact, I'm just getting started." "But do me one favor," Jamie stepped close to Ronnie putting her hands on his face, "Be very very careful." "I love you, and I don't want to be staring down at your grave next." Ronnie hugged her close to him, swallowing the words that would come only in quivering tones.

The funeral was attended by those on the ranch who were Charles friends. When the Richmond Medical Examiner was finished examining Charles body, he was buried in the woods behind his little cabin. The cabin was still taped off as a crime scene. A constant stream of investigators had been in and out of the cabin and woods for most of the month. Chester placed a reward for $50,000 for any information leading to an arrest.

Sophia did not attend the funeral, claiming she was too frightened. To think someone had actually come upon the ranch and committed a murder. She would not leave the house without someone with her at all times. Then making an off-color remark about probable drug dealings which obviously led to the old black man's demise. The remark sent Chester flying at her, and Sophia retiring to the safety of her room.

With the death of Charles came another death, or what felt like the death of the ranch itself. Joy seemed to just melt away from the ranch with his passing. It was eerily quiet all the time. No more dinner parties, the servants crept about like mice avoiding the cat. The main lights stayed off, as did the enormous chandelier above the fourteen-foot dining table that was never used. If anyone ate there at the ranch it was in the kitchen in shifts, avoiding one another. Sadness, darkness, gloom prevailed everywhere. The heart of the ranch quit beating, like that of Charles.

Sophia stayed in her room most of the time when she was home. She hated everyone right now, especially that ill-mannered brute she was married to. There were no simple kind exchanges any longer. Every time they met he glared at her daring her to speak to him, and if she did speak he could not keep a civil tongue in his head; growling and yelling at her, calling her horrible names, making her feel so low. But the worst was Victor. Her heart was broken. How could he treat her in this manner when she had given him her love, her strength, her protection, and of course her money?

He hardly ever came home anymore. She had tried to find him in Richmond, her contacts combing the town of Richmond. She knew where he drank, but he seemed to disappear into thin air at the end of an evening. She just had not found the right people to help her with her dilemma. Most of those that could be hired for the job she wanted to be done were so ignorant, so greedy that she feared for her own existence when employing them for needed duties. She would be patient, all things would come in good time, and she just needed to be patient. She just could not believe everyone was so devastated by the death of the black man. He was just one more low life, expendable, not really worth anything; why then, why?

Victor did stay gone all the time. If he made an appearance once every two weeks or so, it was to gather some of his things and be gone. He usually appeared at night, when he thought everyone was asleep, sneaking up the back entrance, and out within minutes.

"Dad, is that you?" He thought he was hearing things, so kept walking rapidly for the exit. "Victor, wait." He stopped at the top of the stairs and turned to look behind him. It was Jamie, hurrying down the hall toward him. "Please wait." They stood for a moment looking into each other's eyes.

"What is it Jamie?" he asked abruptly.

"Where are you going?".... "Where have you been?" ......"Won't you stay and just talk with me for a few minutes."

"No.," was his answer as began his descent down the back stairway. She reached out and grabbed his arm, the force jerking her off her feet crashing into him.

"What are you doing?" he said exasperatedly.

"Please come into my room and talk with me for just a few minutes, please, please," she begged. "It would mean so much to me, and then I promise to let you go...... no question, you can just go.... and I won't fight you, won't say a word." She was rambling and she knew it. He stood with his head down, shaking it back and forth slowly. He straightened up his stance, took her hand and quickly headed for her room nearly dragging her. He opened her door, pushing her inside looked both ways then stepped in.

"What is it you need to talk to me about?"

"I... I....just need to." "Because you are my father, damn it, maybe you don't love me, but I love you, and right now I need you so much." She was crying now, she could hear herself and hated it. This was not the way she wanted it to be. She wanted to remain calm, self-assured, mature. She was bawling like a newborn calf and could not stop herself. The one human she reached out to since Charles death and rejection was apparent. She sat on the side of her bed holding her hand out for her father. He stood in place. Seconds ticked by without a sound, then surprisingly he walked to the bed and sat beside her. He held her hand caressing it in his, looking down at it like it was a precious breakable item he must protect.

She broke the silence, "where are you staying all the time?" He did not answer, just kept looking down at her hand, rubbing it. She tried again, "I just want to know you are safe."

"I'm safe," he responded softly.

"I love you, I don't want to lose my only other parent," she pleaded. He reached out and pulled her to him, hugging her tightly, kissing her forehead.

"I am sorry I am such a loser." "I just can't be an acting father right now." "I can't even take care of myself." "I guess it is like my mother says, if she is not there to direct me, I am nothing."

Jamie jumped to her feet, "that is not true, you are not like her, she is mean and evil."

He smiled, lightly laughing, "Jamie you need to remember we are talking about my mother, and your grandmother."

"I don't care who she is, it is what she is... a murderer, a witch." "She killed Charles, and most likely my mother; your wife."

He was on his feet, "Jamie that is enough, she is many things, but not a killer."

"Yes, she is and I am going to prove it."

"All right that is enough, I have heard enough." "I am leaving now."

"No, no please don't leave; I am sorry, I won't say anything more about her." "Please stay, I need you."

Victor hugged her briefly again before opening the door and found Sophia standing just outside the door.

He did not waste any time, "excuse me mother, I am late." He headed for the stairway.

"Late for what?" she demanded.

"I'm late," he responded.

"Victor, do not leave this house until you talk with me," she shouted sternly. He reached the stairs racing down them like his tail was on fire.

"Victor!" she yelled. He was gone. "OH," she grunted as she turned to head back to her safe haven. Then noticing Jamie standing in the hall, she began screeching at her like a barn owl in the night. "It's all your fault, ever since you came to this house everything is a nightmare." "You and your whore mother." "I wish you were dead like her," slamming the door to her room.

CHAPTER XV

Ricky Mongo was named after his mother's uncle. What he himself did not know was his mother's uncle was also his father. His mother mostly resenting his birth ignored him, pretending he didn't exist, and leaving his care to her sister, who was too frumpy to make it as a prostitute, so she lived on what Pam paid her to babysit her son. When Pam smacked him around because he was in the way, it was Freda he would run to for protection. Freda was the only one who loved him in the world, his family tree was a bramble bush, and out of the bush, Freda was it. For that reason, it was especially sad when Freda died of cancer shortly after Ricky's eleventh birthday.

With his mother's beauty fading, the money she collected from her pimp minimal, it was not surprising that her addiction had drifted from alcohol to drugs as well. One night shortly after Freda's funeral, mommy crawled into bed with Ricky. She smelled of sour sweat and booze, she fondled him telling him it was her way of making up to him for ignoring him when she had to work so hard to keep them fed.

She used him, poisoned his mind against humanity, and made him believe she was his only lifeline. The only one who had ever cared about him. She taught him how to take drugs and enjoy the feeling. She taught him how to steal, then bring his cache to her. He became her support, her living, and her supplier.

Ricky grew to be exquisitely handsome, almost beautiful; features flawlessly chiseled. His hair was jet black, skin smooth and dark tan in color; often turning women's heads as he walked by them, winking and grinning. He knew how to use them, he knew how to satisfy them; his mother had taught him well. He learned how to market his body and reap the financial benefits. This was much safer than robbing a store, in some cases very pleasurable, and generally paid off well. It kept his mother in booze and drugs, him with new cars, fine clothes, and a new residence; a high-rise penthouse, overseeing his city.

Ricky met Jazzbo near Christmas of his twenty-third year. Jazzbo was a club owner from the

Charlottesville area, he offered Ricky the biggest money yet; a hit, a killing that would net him $20,000 in one night. The hit was the wife of a co-owner of the club. It was so easy, and Ricky found the killing gratifying; her begging for her life and him with the power to snuff it out slow, or fast, however, he chose to commit the deed.

He was hooked; hooked on killing and cruelty, sick with the power of it all, and becoming very rich as well. His mother was drunk 24 hours a day, 7 days a week, which left him with time to build his fortune from blood money. He became known as the east coast's best, fastest, and most accomplished hit man. His prices went up, $40,000 for the average wife, or husband, $100,000 for a politician, or a member of law enforcement, and $150,000 for anyone from the religious order, Freda had taught him some morals.

He was cold, calculating, and smart, without remorse or fear. He could charm the panties off a nun, yet the more resistance he met with, the better the game. The more struggle there was, the more exhilarating the kill was. He was reprehensible and very dangerous.

Sophia had been his most perplexing customer yet. He could not stand this woman. She was rude to him; it was obvious she thought he was scum. If he had his way someday he would choke the life out of her a little at a time. He closed his eyes, and he could see her eyes bulging out of her head, frantically trying to get away, face turning dark blue, pulling at his hands that she could not budge. He started to get an erection. Yes, someday he would get her but right now she was paying him plenty and he would take her money as long as she would give it to him.

Theodore Ames was a banker, one of Sophia's bankers. An account she had set up without Chester's knowledge. Theodore was her friend, so she believed. They lunched often together. One day she made him her confidant, telling him of her miserable existence since Jamie's arrival. "It is not right, Sophia, a handsome woman like yourself in so much pain." "You should be pampered and protected like fine china." She would smile and nod, believing every word knowing that the last thing she ever wanted again was another man to get in her way, but she appreciated the relationship.

It was Ted that introduced Sophia to Ricky. Ted knew of Ricky's abilities, having used his talent to rid himself of an old tottering father, who was senile, making poor decisions, putting a strain on the bank, and their family investments. He would be much happier sent on to his final resting place, and quietly, swiftly, Ricky put him to bed.

Sophia was leaving Leaden Hall for the third time this week. One of the oldest and finest Hotels in Richmond. "What is she doing?" whispered Jamie to herself, as she watched Sophia climb into her limo; holding the door was a driver Jamie had never laid eyes on. Nora told her Sophia had hired a new driver. She said he was not real friendly, talked very little, refused to do anything but drive Sophia wherever she wanted to go and seemed to always be reading a book paying little attention to the world around him. His name was Morrie, mid-thirties, single, and was staying in the apartment in the back of the mansion.

Morrie had trouble walking any distance without the help of a cane. He had multiple birth defects, a twisted spine; elongated appearing head and face; his eyes bulged like some grotesque creature that you would expect to see hanging from a tower in London, peering through the fog down at the humans below. He was quiet, bothered no one and did as he was told, which was all Sophia cared about.

Jamie walked across the street and into Leaden Hall. At the front desk, she asked a distinguished looking gentleman, "sir excuse me, I am Jamie Blackstone, I wonder if you may have seen my grandmother, Mrs. Blackstone?" "I was supposed to meet her, and I was tied up in traffic."

"Oh, my dear, you just missed her." "However, the gentleman she was with is still in the dining area, maybe he could tell you where she was going."

"Could you point him out to me?" "I'd be happy to Ms. Blackstone." As they walked toward the dining area, Jamie's heart began to quicken, it was hard to swallow, her skin was clammy, and it even seemed hard to breathe.

Ricky noticed Jamie walking toward him, even before she knew who he was. The hotel manager turned toward Jamie, "the gentleman facing us on your left, sitting between the column and window; he is dark, quite good looking, wearing a dark blue suit with a red striped tie, his name is Richard Mongo, I will introduce you if you wish." The manager thought Jamie appeared very nervous. "Did you want me to introduce you, Madame?"

"No... I mean...maybe.... ah.... actually, yes that would be nice of you, then I can ask him where she might have gone." Jamie's mouth was so dry her lips seemed to stick to her teeth and the roof of her mouth with every word she uttered. The manager walked toward Ricky with Jamie close behind.

As they approached Ricky, the manager guided Jamie to the front of his stance, "Mr. Mongo, this is Ms. Blackstone, Sophia's Blackstone's granddaughter, she is looking for Sophia, actually was supposed to meet her, isn't that correct Madame?" Jamie nodded, "the lady was wondering if you knew where her grandmother might have gone." Ricky was on his feet pulling out the chair next to him, admiring the woman who stood before him.

"So, you are the granddaughter, how beautiful you are, please have a seat and maybe we can figure out where Sophia may have disappeared." Jamie sat next to Ricky monitoring his every move, as the manager left her in his care. Ricky sat back in his chair tapping his fingers together and gazing at Jamie. "Did Sophia say for you to meet her here at this hotel?"

"Yes, but out in front, we were going shopping." "I was held up in traffic." "We were going to eat lunch." She was so nervous; every sentence seemed to come out in four words or less. He was attractive in a dangerous sort of way. Hair jet black pulled back in a band trailing down his back, but this look seemed to work for him. His eyes were dark brown, almost black in color, a sharp contrast to his white perfect teeth, and smooth tanned skin. Those eyes were piercing, she felt a chill, and an involuntary shiver came over her.

"Hey honey, are you cold?" "Can I get you a sweater or wrap of some kind?"

"No really, it is just the weather." "It seems like it has been raining forever."

"Yeah, it is kind of cold and rainy," he responded. "So, since you missed your lunch with Sophia and neither of us have a clue of her whereabouts, how about you let me buy you some lunch?"

"No, really I am not very hungry."

"Really, well now weren't you just talking about eating lunch with your grandmother?" "What, did I make you lose your appetite or something?" He was grinning, but Jamie felt he really was not amused by her refusal to eat with him.

"Well, all right, I guess it would be ok if I dine with you." "I think I could eat something."

"Good," he said with enthusiasm and with one crack of his hands together, a waiter appeared. "Do you like crab salad?" "They have the best in town." "Yes, that sounds wonderful." "How about some wine, a Riesling '80 would be good?"

"Um, Mr. Mongo," ..."Ricky, please call me Ricky."

"Yes Ricky, I am seventeen, do you really want to serve me wine in here?"

"Seventeen," Ricky said with some surprise. "I would have guessed about twenty-two." "You look so mature and refined." At this, she giggled.

"That is very nice of you, but you know seventeen is actually an extremely short step to being a woman." "I feel I am as much a woman now as I will ever be." This was said in a sexy flirtatious tone. She was gaining confidence, and this encounter felt dangerously intriguing and might yet yield helpful information. Ricky sat smiling at her, taking in the sight of her, already fantasizing about what he would do to her if he had the chance. If she only knew what he had been asked to do to her.

CHAPTER XVI

"So, then what happened, and please do not tell me you did this guy!"

"Of course, not Vicky." "We just sat there and talked about simple stuff, you know the weather and crap." "He is so great looking, but the scariest human I have ever been close to."

"Well honey, if he is scarier than that grandmother of yours, then he must be a real boogie man." "Jamie I am worried about you." "Why are you on this crusade?" "Don't you know how dangerous this is?"

"I know what I am doing Victoria." "And you know damn well why I am on this crusade, as you describe it." "I want to know who killed my mother, and my friend Charles." "Do I believe that it was by Sophia's hand; no." "But what I do believe is she was leading and paying for the hand."

"All right, I can understand your mother, but why Charles, he never hurt anyone."

"Because I loved him that is why." "Because everyone loved him, and she wants to hurt everyone except her son." "Who she believed would come to her like a wounded baby, and instead it backfired." "Now he wants nothing to do with her either." "But she succeeded in one thing; she has fragmented what little family there was." "Do you know I have not seen my grandfather in two weeks?" "It is nearly like my father when he does show his face, he is either working on his books and cannot be disturbed, drunk, or so preoccupied he cannot communicate with me." "He just gets tears in his eyes and hurries off to God knows where." "I have tried to follow him too, but he always loses me."

"Jamie, for someone with a 4.0 you are so dumb."

"What does that mean?"

"Well, now think about it, who knows more about your grandfather than even his own family?"

"Ronnie."

"Right, and if you think Ronnie doesn't know where Chester is spending his nights, you are stupid because you choose to be."

"Do you think he has another woman?"

"Jamie, for God's sake, both your grandfather, as well as your father are attractive men." "I'll bet that old prude Sophia hasn't spread her legs in so long she has cobwebs......"

"Victoria!"

"Well, you know I am right."

"Of course, I do, but you are gross."

"No, she is gross." "Anyway, if I was you I would be pinning down Ronnie baby." "That could be a whole lot more pleasurable, and not so dangerous if you know what I mean."

"You might be right about this, Vicky."

"Jamie honey, you must promise me you won't try to meet this Mongo guy on your own." "It sounds like this guy could really hurt you." Victoria put her arm around her friend, "I love you, my dear, now promise me."

Jamie smiled at her little comrade, hugging her, "I love you too, but I'm not promising anything."

The more Jamie thought about what Victoria had said, she wondered how she could have not thought about this before now. Of course, Ronnie would know where Chester was at all times. Chester was too protective of the ranch to leave the care of it to someone else, and not be available if needed. How to approach Ronnie was the question. Like everyone else, he had been aloof; avoiding the main house altogether, thus Jamie. The last real conversation they had, was at Charles gravesite, and that was weeks ago. She had been so embroiled in her own thoughts and plans, she had pushed that night out of her dreams believing in order to accomplish what she must, the emotions associated with the love of this man must for now be put on hold. She needed to hate, she needed to be as devious as the people who perpetrated the acts against those that she loved.

Jamie did not stop at the house in her car; instead, she drove directly to the barns, to Ronnie's apartment. At first, she did not see his truck, feeling disappointment at possibly missing him; she exited the car and headed for the back corral. There he was, standing in the bed of his truck with a pitchfork in his hands forking out hay to the horses. His hat sat on top of the truck, his shirt was open, and sweat glistened off his brow and chest; he worked diligently. As if by mental telepathy, he looked up like he knew someone was there. He leaned on the pitchfork looking at Jamie standing in the distance. He jumped down from the bed of the truck and walked toward her. The sleeves on the shirt that he wore were cut off at the shoulder seams. What was left of it was blue and white, and seemed to enhance the blue of his eyes. His blond hair fell down over his forehead, his tan well-developed arms rippled each time he moved them. The memory of that night poured over her, and she could feel it everywhere. He walked closer to her and stood quietly for a moment before he spoke. "How are you?"

"I'm ok."

"I'm sorry I look like a sweaty pig here."

"You hardly resemble a pig, and if you did I might consider pig farming." He laughed dropping his head, embarrassed.

"Come here, please," he said with some urgency as he picked her off her feet and hugged her tightly. Her head was swimming as she ran her fingers through his sweaty hair and onto his face, kissing him lightly on the lips. He returned her kiss tenderly but with more force; reminding her he loved her deeply and had missed her. At that moment she pushed him back slightly.

"Ronnie, we need to talk, it is very important." He could see that something was troubling her.

"Come on, let's go in and get something to drink, and we will talk." He led her to his apartment opening the refrigerator he asked, "Well there is ice water, beer, some very old lemonade, and milk." "What's your pleasure?"

"Ice water is fine." He prepared her water and grabbed a beer for himself. They sat at the table in his kitchen, as Jamie tried to find the right words. She couldn't, so she was direct.

"Ronnie, where is my grandfather been staying?" "I know you know where he is, and I want you to tell me." He was about as uncomfortable as he had ever been. He stood and walked across the room staring out the window. Jamie stayed quiet, giving him time.

"I can't tell you that."

"Look, Ron I know he is staying with another woman that is not a problem with me." "I just do not know how to reach my own grandfather, and I need to talk to him."

"I will tell him...."

"No, you will tell me," she stated with as much force as she could muster without yelling it. "He is my grandfather and I have the right to know." "He is the one who insisted I come and live here, and it has been hell since I came." "When I need him the most, he is nowhere to be found." "Now tell me, please."

After a long pause, "I can't tell you, Chester would never forgive me, in fact, he would probably kill me." "If you will just let...." before he could finish Jamie fled his apartment, jumped into her car and sped away sending up a dust storm, scaring the horses. "Damn it!" Ronnie yelled exasperated.

Jamie waited in her room for darkness to envelop the ranch, then walked in shadows to the corral where Ronnie's pickup was still parked. She looked through his window and saw no one. She crouched down hoping he was not somewhere in the dark and had seen her peering in his window. "Well if he has, he has," she said softly to herself. "I need to at least try this." She walked quickly to his pickup, dragging with her a tarp from off the hay bales stacked next to the barn. She crawled into the bed of the truck, covered herself with the tarp, and waited.

She didn't have to wait long, for which she was grateful. It was musty from the recent rains under the tarp, and she was getting hot. Ronnie slid into the driver's side without paying any attention to the tarp, and the truck's engine came to life.

The ride to town presented a significant challenge for Jamie. He was driving very fast, it was extremely difficult to keep the tarp from blowing up where it could be seen, or out of the truck bed altogether, and what was once hot was now very cold with the wind beating down upon her. As her hair blew about in the wind, the dirt and hay in the truck bed blew into her hair sticking there; it flew in her eyes, nose, embedding in the pores of her skin. She was miserable and prayed he was not going far.

Ronnie stopped at the liquor store and then drove on to Erma's residence. Jamie watched as Ronnie climbed the stairs and was let in the door without so much as a knock. She noticed her grandfather's Suburban in the garage and she began to seethe. She walked up the stairs slowly, carefully so as not to make any unnecessary noise. When reaching the top, she stepped to the right of the glass French doors.

She could not believe her eyes. Her grandfather sat at a large kitchen table reading something, smoking a cigar, as a plump woman massaged his neck, and shoulders. He was smiling; he looked very relaxed, enjoying this attention. But what made her boil over was the vision of Ronnie. He was sitting on an overstuffed chair watching television, all the while a dark headed woman kissed his face, rubbed his back and unbuttoned his shirt. He was drinking amber liquid out of a bottle; he was somber, concentrating on the television.

Everyone jumped to their feet when Jamie came bursting through the door, that is except Erma, she plopped down on a bench, mouth agape. After the wild ride in, Jamie resembled an escaped mental patient. Hair standing out everywhere, straw and hay sticking out of it like small lightning rods. Her normal impeccable makeup was smeared with dirt, as was her clothing. She had a crazed look on her face that actually frightened Mary enough that she retreated behind Ronnie.

"What are you both doing?" "Obviously enjoying yourself immensely, leaving me to rot on that fucking ranch, with that old bitch, Sophia!" "You drag me here to live and then abandon me when I need you most!" "You, bastard!" Chester took a step toward her, and stopped at her next statement, "and you, you let me believe you loved me, you made love to me, and I believed you, I believed you!" "God damn you, I hate you both!" She ran from the house, and into the darkness. Chester tried to follow her but was no match for youthful speed.

When he returned to Erma's, Ronnie was sitting at the table holding his head in his hands, Erma trying to comfort him; Mary in the bathroom crying. "Did you take advantage of my granddaughter?" He said slowly in a controlled tone.

Ronnie stood and faced him. "Did I make love to her?" "Yes, I did, because that is what it is, love." "I love her, and I was going to tell you the day I found Charles body." "After that, everything just seemed to fall apart." "I still want to make her my wife."

"Why didn't you tell me before you touched her?" Chester responded now in a raised voice.

"Because I didn't think I was good enough." Chester walked up to Ronnie, nearly nose to nose, grabbing him strongly by the back of his neck. Ronnie winced with pain as Erma pleaded for Chester to stop.

"Get your shit together and get off my ranch tonight!" "If I ever see you again, I'll kill you, do you understand?" Ronnie nodded, gathering his boots, hat, and jacket, then drove away.

Chester combed the streets of Richmond looking for Jamie, but to no avail.

Jamie wandered around until she was under control then called Victoria to help her. "Have you lost your mind?" "You look like someone mauled you." "Are you sure you don't need to go to the hospital or clinic or something?" "Are you bleeding anywhere?"

"No, I don't need to go to the hospital; I need to go home, so I can take a shower." "Please do not lecture me anymore." "I know what I did was stupid, but at least I now know the truth."

"And what is that?" "That Ronnie is human?" "He is a young virile man that you think you can tease and tease and he won't go out looking for someone." "He doesn't love her, he loves you, and you know it." "I just wonder if he is still alive."

"Yeah, I know, I have been thinking the same thing." "My grandfather looked really angry when I said we had slept together."

"God Jamie, I can't believe how stupid you are!"

"All right, all right, just please don't talk anymore, just drive me home in peace." "My head is about to burst." The remainder of the drive was in silence, and when they pulled up to the ranch, Chester's Suburban was parked in front. Before Jamie could get the car door open, Chester was running toward the car.

"Oh God, here he comes Jamie." As she came around the front of the car Chester embraced her.

"Thank God you are safe." "Thank God," he was crying, and Jamie felt like she was going to choke. Her throat felt dry and sore from the ride in Ronnie's truck bed. It was hard to keep from crying herself. She let the rage she felt keep her in firm control. "Thank you, Victoria for bringing her home." "I am so glad you helped her."

"It's ok Mr. Blackstone, she can call me anytime." "I'll always be here for Jamie."

"Thank you again, honey if there is ever anything I can do for you."

"Bye, Mr. Blackstone, by Jamie," as she backed down the drive.

They walked toward the mansion, "Grandfather," "yes honey." "Please don't ask me to talk to you tonight about any of this; I just want to go to my room."

"Of course, I'll walk you to your door," and he did hanging onto her shoulders tightly. When they reached the door, Jamie laid her face on his chest as he picked straw from her hair.

"Please Chester, sleep here, don't leave me alone tonight, even though you are in another room, I will know I am not completely alone."

"Jamie, I promise, I will be right here if you need me." "In the morning, after breakfast, we will go for a long ride, and talk about everything." "Does that meet with your approval?"

"Yes, that sounds fine, but one more thing."

"Yes honey, what is it?"

"Is Ronnie ok?"

"He's fine, Jamie."

CHAPTER XVII

The next morning Chester was waiting for her in the kitchen galley, with a delicious breakfast prepared by a clearly pleased Nora. The conversation was light, avoiding any and all controversial subjects.

The horse ride was most pleasurable, with not one word uttered about the happenings from the previous evening. When returning nearly two hours later to the barns, it was obvious Ronnie was not around. The oats had not been placed in the stalls, and the hay bales not distributed. Chester nervously brushed down his horse and headed for the bin containing oats. Jamie was growing anxious and could not stand this a minute longer, so headed for Ronnie's apartment.

The door was not locked, so she let herself in. Everything seemed normal, yet eerily quiet. It wasn't until Jamie walked to the living room area that her heart sank when she noticed the family pictures no longer sitting on the shelf. She moved toward the bedroom, when momentarily Chester's voice stopped her. "Jamie, what are you doing in here?" She looked at him briefly, continuing into the bedroom. She pulled open drawers, opened the closet door; it was obvious he no longer lived there. His personal belongings were gone.

Chester walked up behind Jamie. "Where is he?"

"I don't know."

"Did you do this?" Complete silence.

Jamie facing Chester, raised her voice, and with a sternness that surprised Chester, "did you force him to leave because he made love to me?"

"Yes."

"What is it with you Blackstone's?" "Must you destroy everyone who comes near you?"

As Jamie stomped from the room Chester attempted to stop her by grabbing her arm. She jerked loose. "How dare you." "How dare you do this!" "You are up in Richmond fucking that fat whore, and you leave me here alone, then deny me any love at all?" "Why?" "Is it your soul intent on making me so miserable that I kill myself?"

"Jamie...Jamie, for God's sake."

"Don't talk to me, you pompous windbag."
"Let's see how you like trying to find me." "You stay here at Tara House, and I will get lost for a while."

Chester's tear-filled eyes suddenly turned cold, "you are not going anywhere, you are not eighteen, and…." Jamie glared at him with as much hatred as she could muster. She could see him begin to retreat, which is all she needed. She bolted from the apartment toward the house.

She hurriedly packed a small bag and ran down the back staircase coming face to face with Morrie at the bottom. For a moment they stood looking quizzically at each other.

"Did you want a ride somewhere?" Morrie asked in a pinched tone.

"Yes, if you don't mind, I want to go to Richmond, and this will be one way."

"You got it, Miss."

There was not a word uttered until they reached Richmond. Morrie asked with gentleness, "Where did you want to go?" This was followed by silence. "Miss Blackstone?"

"Yes....yes." Jamie was absorbed in thought and finally heard Morrie. "Drop me at Mount Carmel."

"As you wish."

Jamie needed time to think. The school would be nearly vacant today, it was Saturday. The Saturday morning class would be out, and all the people left in the building would be the janitors. She needed a quiet place where she wouldn't be disturbed.

Morrie did not have time to exit the limo before Jamie had opened the back door and stepped out. Before shutting the door, she softly said, "thank you sir." "Can we keep this just between us?"

Morrie responded, "Certainly."

Jamie was right; the school was quiet, so she made her way quickly to the main floor bathroom and sitting room. "I need a place to hide out for a few days." "I just need to think this through without anyone influencing me." She talked quietly to her vision in the mirror. "I need a disguise because Chester will be hot on my trail." "That little Morrie won't be able to stand up under Chester's questioning for long." "What to do.....what to do?" She rocked back and forth on the chair as she contemplated her next move.

The bank was not far from the school, and open until noon. There was not even a question when she asked to withdraw $5000 from her account. She had done this before. When she went to California, she took out cash and traveler's checks. She talked about another trip she was taking with her grandfather, and no questions were asked. She knew it would not take Chester long to find the withdrawal, but she would vanish from here.

The closest department store was nearly a mile away, which she walked to swiftly through alleys and back driveways. She purchased a dress; a frumpy flower print dress and some thick black rimmed glasses. She pinned her hair up and put on a scarf. "Now a place to live for a while."

This walk proved to be much longer. Her destination was deeper into the Richmond area, the older area with low-income houses, and shops. She found a small motel that rented two room economy apartments for a week at a time. It was perfect, and if she was very careful about how she moved around the neighborhood; no one would find her.

There was a restaurant across the street still open, and she was hungry. The clientele in Red's Diner were mostly men, and they followed her with their eyes as she walked to the front register ordering a hamburger and cola. The place had obviously been here for many years. It was dimly lit, the paper had begun to peel away from the walls, old floor grease built up around every appliance in the kitchen area. The air from cigarette smoke was suffocating. The man who waited on her had long before lost his front teeth, and in that space hung a cigarette. He grinned at her as she ordered and he kept winking at the men who followed her every move with their eyes. She felt dirty and unsafe so hurried back to her sanctuary to eat.

"Victoria, this is Chester Blackstone, have you heard from Jamie since you dropped her off yesterday?" It was late, nearly midnight on Sunday, and Victoria felt a chill go through her when she heard the sound of Chester's voice.

"No….no I honestly have not."

"Are you sure?" "Can you think of any place she could be?"

"No, not right now.... I mean nothing comes to mind." "She always calls me when she is going somewhere." "No sir, I would tell you." "This makes me a little scared." "It is not like Jamie not to call me, and at least tell me she is alright." "Did you guys have a fight or something?"

"Thank you, Victoria, please call me if you hear from her."

Victoria stood immobile listening to a dial tone, her thoughts racing thinking only if she should have told him about Mongo. Dropping her head slightly she whispered, "Oh please God, let her be alright."

CHAPTER XVIII

Jamie slept very little turning, and tossing; dreaming of running away from an evil force that seemed to pursue her everywhere she went. The room was stuffy, smelling musty, and damp. The night sounds of the country replaced by sounds of traffic, and the all too often the echo of sirens. When she would wake up she would think of the men's faces in the diner, and fear would envelop her. She frequently would get up and check the lock on the door and window, wondering how long she could keep this up. Then she would think of Mary, Charles, Ronnie, her father…. once again, the anger welling up inside of her making her determined to continue with her plans.

The sound of knocking on the door woke her confused and shaken she could not remember where she was. She listened intently to the persistent knocking, finally creeping to the small window to peer out at the individual beating on the door. She recognized the plump gray-headed women who rented her the room. Pulling on a tee shirt from her bag, she opened the door a small crack. "Yes?"

"Mornin Honey, I thought I would bring over some of my fresh cinnamon rolls to my new tenet." "Hey, I am sorry if I woke you." "It is nearly eleven; I thought you would be up by now."

"I didn't sleep well last night." "Thank you so much though, they smell delicious." Jamie reached out through the door crack to recover the rolls. She was shivering. The cool morning air rushing in, and her hair damp with sweat gave her a chill.

"Are you alright honey?" "You are shaking, and you are very pale." "You are pretty young to be here all alone." "You don't look like you belong here either."

Jamie knew she must recover this quickly, or the lady might call the authorities and inquire. She was sure Chester most likely had filed a missing person's report by now; they would be looking for her.

"Listen, what was your name?"

"The name is Maxine." "Maxine Martin and yours is Nancy Beamer?"

"Ah.... yes, that is right, Nancy." "Nice to meet you, Maxine."

"Everyone just calls me Max."

"Ok Max, I will shower and dress, and of course eat some of these great smelling rolls; then I will come over to your office and tell you why I am here." "It's a long story, but really important that you not tell anyone right now." ...... "Ok Max?"

Maxine stood quietly studying Jamie. "Max, I am freezing, would you care if I just take a hot shower now, and I will be over soon?"

"Yeah, ok, I guess that will be fine." "I'll see you shortly then." With that, she turned to go back to her office. She retrieved the morning newspaper to look through it carefully. There might be a reward for someone like her if someone was looking.

Jamie devoured one of the sticky sweet rolls while preparing for her shower. The water pressure was poor, but at the very least it was hot. Jamie put on a frumpy looking sweater and knit pants. Pinning her hair up again, pulling on a knit cap, completing her disguise with the glasses, and heading for Maxine's office.

The office was small, cheery but cheaply decorated. The curtains frilly and obviously sun damaged, covered a large windowpane that was letting in the noontime sun. Maxine stood in a back room, which looked to be the front end of Maxine's living quarters. She was intently ironing a man's shirt. The place smelled of ironed clothes and baked goods. It was cozy and comfortable in a rundown sort of way.

Jamie stood by the front desk waiting patiently for Maxine to notice her presence. In the meantime, she studied the pictures on the wall. They were of another time. A time when Maxine was very young. She was quite pretty and smiling widely from the pictures. She was being embraced by a man, a handsome young man wearing a Naval Seaman's uniform, and between them stood a little blond boy. They looked happy. It looked like ocean waves behind them in the picture.

"Oh, so you're here," Maxine murmured. "You should have said something."

"That's fine; I am not in a hurry." "Is this your husband and son?" "Yes, it is or was."

"What do you mean.... was?"

"Well, my husband was killed about eight years ago." "Run over right out in that very street," pointing to the street in front of the motel.

"My God, how awful." Did you see this happen?"

"No, I heard it though." "Heard these screeching brakes." "Somehow I just knew something bad had happened." "All of a sudden, I just felt numb all over." "You know, how you feel when you lose someone really close, like your mother." "You're not sure where to go or what to do." "Just numb."

"Yes, I do know." "Did they catch the person who did this?"

"He did stop and tried to revive Michael." "He'd been drinking." "Out all night long." "He wasn't very old." "They think he went to sleep at the wheel." "Michael was just going to get a newspaper." "He really didn't suffer, didn't know what hit him." "The kid got manslaughter." "He has two more years left to serve before he gets out." "I don't hold him a grudge though, he's paid." "Him staying in prison won't bring Michael back to me." "Maybe he has learned something, maybe he can help other young kids not to drink and drive by telling his story." She was looking at the floor and talking softly. Talking to herself, as if another human was not in the room. Jamie watched her sadly. Maxine looked to be near seventy. Her face had many lines and wrinkles. She looked very lonely. She wore an old apron-like frock, which made her appear even older.

"Where is your son?"

"He lives in Atlanta." "He is a lawyer," she said with great pride.

"So why do you continue to live here?"

"Because this was our home." "The only home I have known for forty-eight years." "Michael and I bought this motel, about five years after Jonathon was born." "This is where he was raised." "I wouldn't think of moving anywhere else." "I feel close to Michael right here." "Oh, Jonathon has tried to get me to move to Atlanta." "Put me in one of those high falutin condos for retirees." "I'd rather be dead." "All of my friends are here, they live around here." "We check on each other every day."

"Aren't you afraid in this neighborhood?"

"Why would I be?" "You know Miss Beamer, this neighborhood around here, is not bad or dangerous, it's just poor and old, like the rest of us."

Jamie smiled at Maxine. "You're a good person, Maxine." "Do you have any grandchildren?"

"Heavens no." "My son is far too busy for such a thing as children." "She is a lawyer too, so they just work, and fly around the country." "I guess they are happy." "They grace me with a visit about once a year." "They are disgusted with me because I want to live in this rat hole, as Jonathon would call it." "That's fine, let um." "I'm not leaving unless it is time to bury me."

Jamie quietly listened to Maxine and was not prepared for the abrupt change in the conversation. "So, what's your story, Miss Nancy?"

"Well…it is kind of like you would have guessed, I am on the run."

"From the law?"

"No, from my grandfather."

"Is he abusive to you?"

"Yes."

"The son-of-a-bitch." "Sexually?"

"No."

"Well, you can stay here as long as you need to." "But, you don't look like you belong here." "I have a feeling your family ain't the worse for wear." "Even though you are wearing that silly outfit, it doesn't match with you."

"So, whose shirt are you ironing?"

"One of my tenets." "I do his laundry, and several others, for extra income." "I like to cook, and I don't mind the laundry." "Keeps me busy."

"Well, I know where to have my laundry done."

"You planning to stay long, my dear?"

"Actually, no."

"Figured as much."

"Maxine, I just need some uninterrupted time to think about what I am going to do."

"I understand honey." "As I said, you can stay as long as you want."

"So, you won't call anyone?" "You won't tell anyone I am here?"

"No, I wouldn't want some nasty man to hurt you again." "You need to be kinda careful though." "I mean this really is a decent neighborhood, but you are

young and beautiful, and that can be noticed even if
you are trying to hide it." "You never know about
men, one might try to attack you, to have their way
with you." "They aren't going to bother me; I'm just a
fat old lady."

Jamie chuckled at Maxine's comment, patting her
rosy cheeks, "you're a sweet old lady." "I'll be fine."

CHAPTER XIX

It had been a week since Jamie moved into the motel room. She was becoming adjusted and was surprised at her own flexibility. Moving from accommodations like the Blackstone ranch to this little-impoverished motel with so little in her possession and adapting as well as she had; it was commendable. Maxine and Jamie had become good friends talking every day. It reminded her of her relationship with Charles. She so enjoyed listening to Maxine talk about her younger days. She loved Maxine's wonderful home cooking, which she did partake of as often as she was invited.

She found a small drug store two blocks from the motel. It had an old soda fountain, where they sold ice cream, warm roasted nuts, and reading material. Next door was the Goodwill Store where she could buy jeans and tee shirts; she was content to stay as long as needed.

Chester had done exactly as she suspected. He had every lawman, detective, and acquaintance searching the country for Jamie. There was a $100,000 reward for information leading to the safe return of Jamie to Chester Blackstone.

Everyone now knew of her disappearance. Aunt Audrey, Alex, Ronnie, Victoria, searched endlessly, calling everyone ever associated with her. But she seemed to have disappeared into thin air. No one had seen her, and Morrie…. Morrie had refused to tell anyone anything. He simply stated, he had gone to town to get an oil change in the limo, and never saw Miss Jamie. No one questioned him further.

Ronnie called the ranch on several occasions, but when Chester answered, his questions concerning Jamie ended abruptly with the sound of a dial tone. If Nora or James answered the telephone was the only time he could get any information on the search for Jamie.

Ronnie was sick most of the time. He couldn't eat or sleep. He paid a local rancher from the Richmond area who he knew he could trust $10,000 for his silence and a good horse. He combed the area between the Blackstone ranch and Richmond step by step looking for any clue to Jamie's whereabouts.

Alex did the same only by helicopter, and with Chester's blessing.

"Do you know who she is?" "She's a Blackstone!" "That old man Blackstone has more money than God!"

"Yes, I know who she is!" "What business is this of yours anyway, you little shit!"

"$100,000, that is what it is about." "If you don't need that money, me and my mom could use it!"

"If you tell anyone she is here, I will blow your little ass away!" "Do you understand me?"

"Yeah, Yeah, Yeah, I hear ya, Maxine." "But if you think I am the only one thinking about that money, you're dead wrong." "Everyone who's seen her is thinking about it."

"Get the hell outa here, I don't want to hear any more about this," Maxine yelled. As she watched him walk away, she thought to herself out loud, "I have never liked that kid, I don't trust him, and I'm going to call the newspaper and tell them I want a new carrier." "The little bastard."

When Jamie returned from her daily walk to the drugstore, there was a note hanging on the door,

"ROOM FOR RENT, CHECK AT THE OFFICE FOR INFORMATION." She thought at first, she might have the wrong room. No, number five on the door. She peered through the window and could see the room was made up, and her things appeared to be gone. She headed for the office.

As Jamie stepped into the office door, Maxine came from her residence with a frightened look in her eyes. She waved frantically at Jamie to come into her room. As Jamie stepped into her apartment, Maxine slammed the door shut behind her. "You have got to get out of here," she whispered sternly.

"Why, what is going on?"

"They know you are here."

Jamie could feel herself losing color and growing panicky. "Who is they?"

"The law, your grandfather."

"How do you know this?"

"They've been here and called." "That damn brat paperboy turned you in for the money." "Little bastard."

"So where are they now?"

"I told them you checked out this morning, and they believed me."

"Did they check the room?"

"Yes, but I had already taken your stuff, and it is under my bed."

"Why did you do that?"

"Because the little bastard had already threatened to turn you in, and I just had a feeling."

Jamie threw her arms around Maxine's neck and hugged her tightly. "Oh my God, I owe you so much, Maxine."

"You need to get out of here and stop tempting me."

Jamie hugged her again, "you will be repaid, I promise you." Jamie retrieved her bag from under Maxine's bed and tried to give her $1000, but Maxine pushed it away.

"Young lady, you need to get on the road, and take your money with you." "I am an old lady; I really don't need it where I am going."

"You're not going anywhere for a long long time."

"Uh huh, now listen, I have an old friend Joe, who don't need no money either." "He will be here in a minute." "He has a brown pick-up truck, and he is going to give you a ride to the train station."

"His brother is one of the conductors." "He has a baggage car you can ride in, and he will make sure there ain't no Hobos or rats or anything in the car." "You can ride the train to Portsmouth, and then it's up to you from there."

They both jumped at the sound of a vehicle pulling into the drive. Maxine looked through the window, "it's him, you need to go."

Jamie grabbed her bag that Maxine had packed, hugged and kissed the old lady on the cheek, "thank you, thank you, my friend."

"Yeah, Yeah, go on now, just keep in touch."

Jamie ran to the pick-up and slid in on the dilapidated seat next to an obese black man, with a large cigar in his mouth, and a fedora on his head. "So, you are Miss Jamie?"

"Yes, sir."

"Well hang on Miss, we are in a hurry."

Jamie closed her eyes tightly as the truck raced through the streets of Richmond toward the train station. As they reached the station, Joe pulled the truck behind the station as close to the train as he could get, but in the shadow of darkness. As they exited the truck he began counting the cars, and on the sixth car, he motioned Jamie to follow him. The door was open, and no one was around. "Now you climb up into the baggage car, which was full to capacity." "Here, you might need this along the way." Joe handed her a small gun.

Jamie looked at him helplessly. "I've never shot a gun like this before; I have no idea......"

"Look, all you have to do is pull back like this, and a bullet is in the barrel." "Then you flip this up, see the red dot that means the safety is off and it is ready to shoot." "It is an automatic nine shot loaded; you should be able to stop most anything with it." "Here's how you disarm it." "You got it?"

"Yes, I think so."

"Alright I'm giving you a hand up and you climb into this car." It was a struggle with her bag but Jamie managed to get into the car.

"Looks like they are getting ready to pull out." "You take care, now ya hear?"

"Thank you, Joe." "I will never forget your kindness." "Can I give you some money?"

Shaking his head "no," he waved to her as he hurried back to his truck.

Jamie slid down to the floor of the car placing her hands over her face, and rubbing her eyes whispering, "what just happened?" "I cannot believe I am here." A loud bang nearly made her urinate in her pants, as the door to the car was slammed shut. It was pitch black in the car, "Jesus." She whispered loudly. She fumbled in her bag looking for the small flashlight she had packed before leaving the ranch. The car was cold; she managed to find a packing blanket and a large soft leather trunk which she curled up on. Turning off the flashlight to save the batteries, she could see light coming through the cracks on the side of the car. The rocking of the train lulled her to sleep, which seemed a very short period of time before the loud bang woke her again.

Someone was pulling some of the baggage out of the car. She could hear men talking; she stayed hidden in the darkness. Then someone with a soft male voice said, "Miss...Miss, are you in there?" Well, whoever it was, knew she was supposed to be there. She stood and walked to the door. An older man in a conductor's hat stood just outside the door. He was looking both ways, "this is Portsmouth." "You wanted to get off here, right?"

"Yes, I do." She threw her bag out and then jumped down from the car.

He smiled at her slightly, "I can't imagine what a girl like you is doing here, and I don't want to know." He motioned toward the station. "You can get a taxi, or if you need a phone, in there." "Good luck."

"Thank you, sir," she began walking toward the station, her bag slung across her back. The conductor walked off in the opposite direction, shaking his head and muttering to himself.

Jamie looked at the phone book in an old booth, just inside the station. There weren't many people there, so she took her time. She looked for a hotel near the airport. There was a Traveler's Inn not far from the airport, she wrote down the address so she could instruct the taxi driver exactly where she wanted to check in. The hotel was closer then she anticipated; right over the hill and up the road from the station. She wore her glasses so he would have more difficulty recognizing her. She did the same at the Traveler's Inn, however, knew she would not have a problem there, as the sleepy disinterested girl who checked her in could have cared less who she was.

It was nearly midnight by the time she reached her room. She called the front desk to ask for a wake-up call. After a hot shower, she crawled into bed naked, with a towel wrapped around her wet hair; in seconds she was asleep.

CHAPTER XX

At first, there was a feeling of something crawling lightly on her skin. Just a little irritating, not even enough to make her want to stir, or completely wake up. Then silence, drifting back to warmth and a fluffy serene dream world. Suddenly three senses going off like a large display of fireworks on the fourth of July. The loud jingling of the telephone, the feel of cold steel on the middle of her bare back, and the smell of cigarette smoke mingled with sickeningly spicy cologne. Jamie jerked herself up, turning toward her right. Fear gripped her as she faced Ricky Mongo setting on the bed next to her, holding what appeared to be a large knife. He was smiling looking directly at her exposed breasts, and murmuring, "my...my...what do we have here?"

The phone was still ringing. He carefully lifted the receiver off of the base putting it next to Jamie's ear. Simultaneously placing his finger over his lips. She could hear the recording telling her it was 7:00am.

Life is an inner journey for every person who lives for any length of time. All feelings and emotions are experienced at one time or another. How each person learns to accept what is awarded them or taken from them, is some intuit determination of what will become of them in the future yet to arrive. Some may be surrounded by love, others, none. Some grow filled with hate and rage against those who did not complete their parental bonding, creating the right mix of what was required to produce a stable and self-assured adult. Then there are those who simply do not care about the human experience, for others or themselves. They are driven only by self-gratification. Nothing shames them, hurting others physically or mentally is not a concern. In fact, often, it is stimulating and pleasurable. They are afraid only of not getting what they want and protest loudly if not awarded what they quest. Imprisonment and denial of their need is the greatest punishment for their actions. Not even death is worse. Extremely smart, driven to succeed, they often end up as leaders. Cunning and manipulative, others follow with dedication in their misguided cause. They cannot be rehabilitated. More intelligent than those who attempt to help them, they tear through life filling up like a glass under a waterspout with all that pleases them, leaving the victims behind.

The image in the mirror appeared to be a stranger. Drawn and tired, pale nearly devoid of her normal color, Jamie stared at herself. Her eyes were swollen from crying. Her back hurt. When examining the damage, the cut extended the full length of her back. Deeper then she thought at first. Dried blood crusted on the edges, running in various directions like the main river and its tributaries. It felt like someone was rubbing soap into the center. Every time she moved pain shot through her like a red-hot poker. "Oh God, please help me." She sat down hard on the toilet, and rested her head on the sink, sobbing. The phone silenced her. Jamie's heart was beating hard and fast, her breath caught in her throat. The phone continued to ring. Slowly she rose and walked to the phone. Numb, she picked up the receiver and held it to her ear. "Miss Simmons?" "Hello." "Miss Simmons?"

It took Jamie a few seconds to remember Melissa Simmons was the name she registered under the night before. "Yes."

"Miss Simmons, will you be checking out today?"

Jamie looked at the clock, it was 12:15. Checkout was 12:00. "Ye...Yes...I mean." Jamie gazed at the carpet covered with blood. "I mean I will be staying for another day." "I am exhausted, and I am not feeling well, so I am going to sleep in today." "Um, my plane tickets to California are not for two more days, and I can't think of a nicer place to stay and recoup."

"Well, I thank you for the compliment," Jack Spade, the hotel manager said smiling to himself. "Is there anything I can get for you, to make you more comfortable?"

"Actually, there is." "I need more towels, and I won't be needing the maid to clean the room, I prefer no one to come in until I check out." "Also, can I get some soup, and maybe some hot coffee?"

"Of course, I can arrange both, but first we need to clear up a little matter." Jamie felt a chill.

"What is the problem?"

"You checked in after hours, and you paid cash, which is fine." "However, if you are going to stay another day, we will need you to secure this room with a credit card or pay for the room in cash now." "I am sorry about the inconvenience, especially if you are not feeling well, but it is hotel policy."

"That is fine, I understand." "Would you mind if I shower first before coming down to pay you?"

"I will be glad to deliver the towels to your room now, and you can pay me then." "Will, that be more convenient for you?"

"I do not mean to sound rude sir, but I really need a woman to deliver the towels." "You see I had a little accident last night while sleeping." "A female kind of accident, if you know what I mean." "I don't mean to be difficult, I am just embarrassed."

Silence…which seemed to linger. "Of course, Miss Simmons I will send up the maid immediately with more towels and washcloths." "I will transfer you to room service, and you can order what you like, they will bring it up, and it usually takes about fifteen minutes." "You can just come to the front desk and pay for your room when everything is in order." He was stumbling over his words. "Just leave the cash with the girl at the front desk, I will tell her you will be coming." "But take your time." "Does that meet with your approval?"

"Thank you so much for understanding."

"Yes, I am transferring you now." Jack hung up the phone, disgusted. "Why would anyone question why I like men?" He muttered to himself, hurrying to his office.

Jamie ordered clear chicken soup and hot coffee. The maid appeared within minutes with an arm full of towels and sheets. "Hi, what is your name?"

"Evelyn." "Is there anything else I can get for you?"

"Yes Evelyn, there is." "You see I get heavy unpredictable periods." "Maybe because I am so exhausted and sick, but I bled all over the sheets, and I am afraid it soaked through." "Could I get some liquid soap from you, so I can clean everything off?"

"Heavens no, that is my job, I'll clean it for you."

"No, please Evelyn, I really feel awful about this." "It is not that big of a deal, but I would rather do it myself, I am so embarrassed."

"You know this is a natural thing, we all been through it, Missy." "I really don't mind none."

"Look if you are worried that I won't do a good enough job......"

"No, that is ok Miss; I am just trying to do my job."

"I know you are, and I don't mean to sound so bitchy, I just don't feel well, and I want to bathe."

"Look if you will just keep this between us girls." Jamie was fumbling through her bag retrieving the money. She handed Evelyn forty dollars. "Now if you would just come back in a couple of hours to pick up the towels I would appreciate it."

Evelyn looked at the forty dollars in her hand. "You must want to scrub that bed yourself really bad." Then shrugged her shoulders, "I got no problem with that," as she slid the money into her pocket. "I'll be back in two hours."

Jamie forced a smile at Evelyn, "make it two and a half and where are the washers and dryers?" "I have some things I want to wash." Evelyn nodded toward the end of the hall, "last door on the right, you will need your key," and walked down the corridor.

Just as Evelyn turned toward the exit, a young man came walking up the hall with Jamie's tray. She tipped him, placed the Do Not Disturb sign on the door, and double locked it. Shaking so hard she was not sure she could pour the coffee into the cup, she once again reached in her bag for the bottle of Tylenol she had packed. She drank as much of the soup and coffee as her irritable stomach would tolerate. Then she headed to the bathroom for a warm shower.

CHAPTER XXI

The bloody mess was difficult to clean. At times an overwhelming job leaving Jamie nauseated, from the sickening smell of the blood. Time after time she would run to the bathroom to vomit. She had forgotten to ask for gloves, and unable to find any in the janitor's closet down the hall she continued her task without the assistance of gloves. She prayed he didn't have some horrendous disease she might contact.

"That would be my luck," she whispered under her breath as she scrubbed the carpet over and over. The only remote bit of luck in all of this was he didn't bleed into the mattress. The blood that was on the sheets was her own.

There was so much blood. He had lost so much blood. Every time she thought she had cleaned the carpet completely, the pink-tinged liquid would squish up between her toes when she would walk on the wet carpet. She was approaching exhaustion, and she still had to get rid of his body. It would be days before this cockroach would be missed, she was sure of it.

Her mind whirled constantly as she made her many trips back and forth with the soapy water. She had opened the windows as far as she could and turned up the fan and heat in the room to the maximum setting, hoping it would improve the drying time and odor of death that pervaded the room.

She had managed to drag him to the bathtub and push him over the edge so he was lying face down in the tub bleeding out the remainder of his body fluids into the drain. Jamie had decided she could not get him downstairs by dragging him. It would only take one door opening a crack to expose her crime. She would take her chances with the window.

Jamie had been staring out the window watching the trains pull in and out of the station when she began to form a plan in her mind. It was necessary that she stay in this nightmare another day, long enough to complete the cleaning of the room, making sure the carpet was completely dry and tying up any loose ends. Most of this must be completed under the cover of darkness; she would sleep if possible during the day.

He had a car somewhere around here; she needed to find it. He owned several if his bragging was to be believed, and she was sure it was. His keys were in his pocket, along with $4,030. She would walk around the building and try every car if necessary until she found it, she knew whatever it was it would be an expensive one. She had to have that car to complete her plan.

The parking lot just on the other side of the bushes outside her terrace contained what she was looking for; a black Lexus. She drove to the edge of Portsmouth, to an all-night grocery store, purchasing food, disposable gloves, cleaning solution, a small bucket, cleaning cloths, tape, and garbage bags. As she returned to the room, she parked as near to her window as she could get. There was a keyless code entry door in the back of the hotel she planned to use.

When Jamie returned to the room she paid close attention to the traffic around the building. It was dark, a little after 9:00pm, and relatively quiet. She would be patient. She shut the bathroom door and proceeded to devour some of the food she purchased. She sat quietly watching the television and drinking some hot black coffee she had made in the room. She was extremely fatigued and ached all over especially her back, she murmured "God, please don't let my back get infected." Laying her head down on the armrest of the couch, she drifted off to sleep.

The pain in her back....

"why are you doing this, what do you want?" He placed his hands over her breasts and squeezed. She jerked violently away. He was now on top of her pinning her down, rubbing, pinching, violating her in every way.

"I am going to fuck you, then I am going to kill you, and enjoy every moment.... then I get paid."

Jamie screamed, "Why Ricky, why...what have I done to you?" Crying, twisting, and fighting for her life, feeling absolute terror.

"Too bad I didn't get to do this to your hot mamma before she took a bullet to the head." Jamie was stunned into silence. "That old nigger was almost a waste of my time, so I decided to enjoy that one." "Like a barnyard cat with a mouse they are too full to eat." "Just play with them till you're sick of it, then bite their heads off." He bent forward and clicked his teeth in her face. That was all the edge she needed. Jamie raised her knees and fists, hitting with both at the same time throwing him off balance and knocking him to the floor. The knife dropped next to him as Mongo scrambled to catch himself. Jamie grabbed the knife and rolled off the other side of the bed. He lunged back over the bed falling into an already poised knife, severing the front half of his aorta. He gasped grabbing at Jamie, eyes wild and desperate, unbelieving like there was some sort of terrible mistake and he expected her to fix it. She sat a foot away from him, watching him reach out sputtering and gurgling until his eyes rolled back in his head, and he died.

The sound of a car engine woke Jamie. She was shaking, freezing cold, yet dripping in sweat. She jumped to her feet, "what time is it?" It was nearing midnight. Whatever car engine started or stopped, it was quiet outside now. Not a movement anywhere. Now was the time.

Even though most of his blood volume was lost, rigors had developed. He was extremely heavy and hard to handle, especially for someone half Mongo's size. Pulling and tugging, Jamie managed to drag Mongo over the side of the tub and onto large black industrial size garbage bags. She wrapped his frame with the bag and black electrician's tape she had purchased at the store. She then began pulling him inch by inch toward the window. Once out on the small terrace getting him over the railing and dropping him onto the concrete without anyone seeing anything would simply be a game of chance.

Getting Mongo over the railing was not as hard as she had anticipated. He was top heavy and with the rigors made it easy to maneuver him over the side. He fell with a thud in the bushes. Jamie knelt down and was very still checking for any movement. Minutes passed, but no sign that anyone had noticed or heard the fall.

Jamie moved swiftly down the stairs and out the back door. It was a beautiful clear crisp night; the stars were shining brightly. Momentarily Jamie drifted back to the ranch, looking at the stars from her balcony. As she began dragging Mongo toward the car she remembered something else, something her mother would say, "when we practice to deceive, what a tangled web we weave." Out loud in a whisper, she said, "no shit!" "Web my ass, more like a tangled bunch of black bars I will be behind."

Jamie's largest struggle was to get Mongo's body in the trunk of his Lexus. Time and time again she would get his top half nearly in the trunk, only to have him slip back onto the ground. At one point she heard a car pull up. A couple unloaded suitcases and walked into the back door of the hotel. Jamie lay quietly on the ground next to Mongo's body until it was once again quiet. She was crying, she had not even realized she had been crying until she stood up and could feel the cool breeze on her face. She wiped her face, and muttered, "I can do this." She struggled again, this time with him hanging halfway in and out of the trunk. Again, she gave another shove and managed to push him into the trunk.

Knees quivering, she slowly and quietly as possible started the car and coasted toward the road. Jamie drove near the station around the back-entrance road and pulled off into the darkness.

Getting Mongo's body out of the trunk was considerably easier than getting him in. She drug him to the driver's side of the car. She began cutting away the black plastic and tape. Placing Mongo behind the wheel of the car was her second greatest challenge. First of all, his face was now swollen and grotesque. His skin felt slimy, and he was starting to stink. Again, Jamie was sick. Her head was throbbing, nausea enveloping her every minute. She could hear a train and see the light. She had to move.

Once the door on the driver's side was closed she slipped into the passenger side and started the engine, slowly rolling toward the train tracks. When on the tracks she placed the car in neutral and jumped out running into the bushes. Within seconds the train was closing in on the vehicle. The train conductor began sounding the train's whistle and applying the brakes. The screeching sound of metal sliding on metal, sparks flying everywhere, and then the crash followed by an explosion. The car had burst into flames, and the train continued to push the car which was now a blazing inferno down the tracks, with pieces of metal and sparks soaring everywhere until the train came to a complete stop.

Jamie was running, running with what energy she had left back to the hotel. She did not even look back. She could hear the echo of men's voices calling for emergency vehicles and help to put out the flames.

Even though the crash and the explosion were deafening, there was not even a stir at the hotel. Jamie was able to slip in the back door, and up to her room without notice. She collapsed on the couch she had made into a bed and did not move until the expected ring of the phone at 7:00am.

"Ms. Simmons, this is Mr. Spade, hotel manager, I am sorry to bother you, but you did not ask for a wake-up call, and I know you have been ill." "I actually called to see if you are any better."

"No, I am not better." "I was up all night, I am nauseated, headache…. I think I have the flu." "I was actually trying to get some sleep."

"Well again, Ms. Simmons, I do apologize for waking you." "Do you need a physician?"

"No Mr. Spade, but I am going to stay another day to rest and I will be down to pay you." "I will be leaving by 9:00am in the morning, and I will need a taxi to the airport."

"Very well Ms. Simmons, is there anything else I can get for you?"

"Yes, I will need Evelyn to bring more towels, and some coffee please." "Also, could you switch me over to room service?"

"Of course, Ms. Simmons, I hope you soon feel better."

The breakfast Jamie ordered sat cold and untouched. Unable to eat, or sleep any longer Jamie continued her meticulous cleaning of the room. She could think of nothing other than how she would formulate plans on finding who had hired Ricky Mongo to kill her. Why he would have known her mother and have anything to do with her death at that time. Why Charles? Why.... Why, where to go from here? How did he know where she was?

CHAPTER XXII

Thoughts running through her head, "I was defending myself, why is it murder?" "He killed my mother, but why would he, who paid him?" "The damn light is so bright.... I need to turn it off."

Opening her eyes, the light was the morning light. The sun was up, and the breeze was cool coming off the ocean. It felt so good on her hot skin. Her skin was very hot, she felt her face, it felt like a bad sunburn. She pulled the towel off her head. Her hair was still damp from the shower. That felt even better. Now she was nauseated, and her head was pounding. She tried to stand but began to retch from nausea, a blessing that she had nothing in her stomach. Again, she struggled to her feet, waves of dizziness and nausea overcame her, she dropped to her knees. "Oh God, I am so sick," holding her hot forehead in her hands, and crying softly. She lay back down on the deck, "is this how I am going to die, like an overripe tomato in the sun, all swollen and grotesque?"

Jamie thought of Mongo and the things he said about killing her mother. "Too bad I didn't get to do this to your hot mamma before she took a bullet to the head." "That old nigger was almost a waste of my time."

The only reason Mongo would waste his time on her mother or Charles; he was paid well, but who and why? It just did not make sense that Sophia would have both her mother and Charles eliminated.

The thoughts seem to generate energy within Jamie, and she began to crawl toward the French doors. I must know who ruined all our lives. "I refuse to die until I know," Jamie said aloud.

CHAPTER XXIII

"God I can't even move." "I feel like a big fat bug on its back." ……. "Look at him, looking all slim and trim." "The bastard, I hate him, I hate this kid growing inside me like an alien, and all he thinks about is that Blackstone bitch." "I don't care what he says, I know it, I can feel it." "I don't know why he stays." "He can give me half his money, and I will leave this God forsaken place." "Bastard!"

The voice in Mary's head of late was one consumed by anger and frustration. This place in Wyoming was lonely, she was uncomfortable, and missed Erma's place. Erma had been like her second mom. Her only mom, since her mother never cared if she survived childhood, let alone adolescence. Like Ronnie was treating her right now. He never talked to her, just muttered. He was miserable, it was obvious and she knew why.

"Ronnie, what is the matter with you today?" "You been in and out of that front door at least a dozen times in the last hour." No answer. "Ronnie!"

"What is it?"

"You act like it is an inconvenience to even answer me." "I'm just not good enough for you, am I?" "All fat and pregnant with your kid," shouted Mary.

"Shit women, will you shut up?" "I am so tired of listening to you whine and bitch."

"Why shouldn't I whine?" "I am miserable."

"Why did you get pregnant in the first place?" seethed Ronnie. "You were an expert at being a whore, so how is that possible?"

"So, I could trap you right?" "So, you would always owe me for the kid," sobbed Mary. "That's what you think, right?"

Ronnie turned toward her dropping his head, "look I don't think that." "I......

Mary shouted, "you just want me to go away or die, so you can go to that Blackstone bitch." "She's probably dead since no one can find her."

With that statement Ronnie turned and marched out the door to his truck making a dust storm exit away from the ranch and to the nearest bar. This was a frequent scene played out nearly every day, both people unhappy with their lives as well as each other, but neither willing to just walk away.

"Erma?"

"Mary, is that you?"

"Yes, it's me."

"You two been fighting again?" "You sound like you been crying."

"That is all we do anymore, is fight," lamented Mary. "I can't stand this anymore." "I hate him, I hate this place, I am so miserable."

"Well honey, you know I would invite you here, but Chester would not like it." "I might be able to find you a place in the area, and him not know." "That Ronnie, you know has some money." "He might be willing to support you if you agree to split and come here." "I could help you then, Chester wouldn't have to know, at least not right away." "I feel so bad for you." "I am sorry you are going through this all alone." "Does he know they found her?"

"What are you talking about?" "Found who?"

"Jamie Blackstone, they found her."

"You are kidding, where?"

"At some beach house in California." "She is really sick, in the hospital in L.A." "I guess she is septic they said, from some infection." "Chester left yesterday, someone called him." "So, I take it Ronnie does not know."

"No, Ronnie doesn't know, he would be gone." "If I was in labor he would still be gone."

"Are you going to tell him?"

"I don't know, maybe."

"You would be better off here, Mary." "He would probably agree, I mean you are carrying his child."

"Yeah, I need to think about things, I will call you back." "She might die?"

"She must be really sick." "Chester said she was on life support."

"I will call you back Erma."

"OK, honey, bye now."

Mary was calmer inside then she had been in weeks. She was finally blessed with some good fortune. A chance to go home where at least one person cared for her, a chance to hurt Ronnie as he had hurt her, and maybe, yes maybe even a chance he would be hers completely with no one else in the picture because Jamie Blackstone may die. She would wait and think on just what to say.

Mary waited all night for the sounds of the truck pulling into the drive. The next morning, she made fresh coffee and waited. At 9:00am she called the sheriff.

"Well I might know where I can find him, I saw his truck downtown this morning," of course you did, sneered Mary to herself.

"If you can find him, Sheriff Tim, tell him it is important, to come right away."

"Will do mam."

Mary sat at the kitchen table smiling to herself. She marveled at the fact she was awake all night and was not the least bit tired. It wasn't long until she heard Ronnie's truck pull in the driveway. She glanced at herself in the mirror, trying to seem somber, and exhausted. Ronnie came in the door with a concerned look on his face. His eyes were red-rimmed and puffy, obviously hung-over.

"Are you alright?" "Sheriff Tim said you needed me right away."

"I am tired, but I am fine." "You should set down."

"Alright, I am down, what is wrong?"

"I talked to Erma this morning, and they found Jamie Blackstone."

Ronnie sat frozen in his seat, not moving, not blinking, "and..."

"She is in an L.A. hospital, and is near death, some sort of an infection."

Ronnie stood and walked to the kitchen window with his back to Mary. Neither spoke for a long period of time.

Mary broke the silence, "I can go stay in Richmond, Erma said she would get me a place." "I want to be there, not here." "Then you can go and do what you want." "We will both be happier." "I just need some money since obviously, no one would hire me like this, and in my previous profession it might…."

Ronnie interrupted her, "I will arrange your immediate move." "Just ask Erma when you can move in." "In the meantime I'll book you a suite in a nice hotel." "You call the doctor's office and get copies of your records." "Pack your things." "You can get a doctor when you get there." "I will take care of all your expenses and send you money to live on."

"You will never need to work." "But after the kid is born, get yourself a lawyer." With that, he walked out the door. Mary sat in silence.

CHAPTER XXIV

"Did you love her?"

"Excuse me, Mr. Blackstone, the question should really be, do I love her, and the answer would be, yes always."

Alex sat on a chair next to Jamie's bed, holding her hand occasionally putting his forehead on her arm. Chester stood at the foot staring helplessly at the ventilator that controlled her breathing. Normally Chester would have continued to probe Alex about his and Jamie's relationship, but not today. He felt weak and old. He wanted so much to help her but knew this was one time he was not in control. He could not even bring himself to walk to her side, and speak to her, kiss her, or even hold her hand. Alex was there when he arrived, sitting right where he was now. Chester stood like his feet were mounted in cement at the foot of Jamie's bed.

Due to her septic condition, Jamie was in an isolation room in Intensive Care. Everyone entering the room was required to wear a hat, gown, and gloves. The bacteria had not yet been confirmed, so the hospital was taking no chances in spreading the infection to others.

Soon a young nurse stepped into the room. "I am going to ask you, gentleman, to step out now for about 30 minutes. I will be drawing some blood, and doing her PM care so I will let you know when you can come back to see her." They both nodded their heads.

"Also, there seem to be quite a few family members showing up in the waiting room." "Please share with them that only two members can visit every hour for fifteen minutes."

Chester looked puzzled. Alex responded, "Of course, we will tell everyone."

"Thank you," she said smiling and holding the door as they exited.

Alex and Chester were surprised when they reached the ICU waiting room. It was full of people spilling out the front door. The charge nurse walked up behind them, gently putting her hand on each man's shoulder. "Hi, I am Patty Schumacher, I am the evening charge nurse." "Because there are so many family members for Jamie here, and because she is one of our most critical, we have opened up another waiting area for your family." "Our ICU is full tonight, so this way everyone will have a seat." "Will, that meet with your approval?"

"This is very kind of you Patty, thank you," Alex quietly responded.

Chester just smiled and nodded. It was obvious that Chester was overwhelmed, and now having difficulty maintaining control of his emotions.

"Chester,"

"Yes,"

"Before we go into this Blackstone waiting room I want to share one thing with you,"

Chester looked into Alex's eyes and nodded. Chester's eyes were now filled with tears, his chin quivering. Alex placed his arm around Chester's shoulder and spoke softly in his ear, "no matter who is in there because you and I both know few if any are true family members; remember they are all here because they love Jamie, and how would she want you to treat them?" "She would want you to treat them like the family that is how she thinks of them." "Some of these people she loves dearly."

Chester put his head in his hands and sobbed. Alex stood quietly continuing to keep his arm firmly around Chester's shoulders. Patty came with tissue, then led Chester and Alex toward the waiting room now filled with Blackstone family members and friends.

The room was full. The only person Alex knew was Audrey. He immediately walked to her and embraced her. "Alex, what happened to her?" Tears running down Audrey's face.

"I don't think any of us really know at this point."

Chester immediately noticed Ronnie standing by a window. He walked swiftly over to him, as Alex braced himself. Chester held his hand out to Ronnie and said, "thank you for coming." Ronnie grabbed Chester's hand in a firm grip pulling him forward and embracing him.

"How is she?" Ronnie spoke in a choked response.

Chester shook his head, dabbing his eyes, "I really don't know." "The nurse said she was the most critical of all the people in this ICU."

Ronnie stood quietly with his head down, trying his best to fathom this. "What happened?"

Again, Chester shook his head, unable to answer. Alex watched this exchange thinking to himself, "thank God Chester is behaving himself."

The room fell to a soft hush when a doctor and nurse entered. Chester turned to see who was there. Directly behind the doctor and nurse entered an obviously very distraught Victoria, with her parents.

"Excuse me, my name is Dr. Williams." "I am looking for the immediate family of Jamie, and what I mean by immediate, is father, mother, grandfather, grandmother, and anyone they deem acceptable to talk with me about her condition."

Chester walked to the doctor with his hand extended, "Dr. Williams, I am Chester Blackstone, Jamie's grandfather."

The doctor warmly shook Chester's hand, "good to meet you, sir." "I would like to talk privately with you and other members you would permit to hear about her condition." "However, I would like you to keep that number at around five, simply because there is a good deal to absorb, and the remainder of the members should be told only that information that the family chooses to share." "Also, the room we will be talking in is small." "Some of the subject matter will be hard to understand, and sensitive for Jamie and your family, which is another reason to keep it intimate."

Chester nodded, "of course." He then turned and motioned toward Alex and Audrey. He also put his hand on Ronnie's shoulder, again nodding.

As Chester, Alex, Audrey, and Ronnie followed Dr. Williams down the hall, Victoria followed close behind. When reaching the conference room, Victoria clutched at Chester's shirt. He turned to look into her swollen red eyes, she whispered, "please." Chester put his arm around Victoria and stepped into the room with her under his arm.

Dr. Williams began by introducing his nurse as Miss Rivers. Just as he positioned himself resting on the edge of a desk facing the seated group, the door swung open, "this is a closed conference sir; can I help you?"

A pale Victor Blackstone stood in the doorway, "I am her father."

The Dr. looked at Chester for his response, which was slow because he was staring disbelievingly at

Victor. Chester nodded his head, as Victor took a chair among the group.

"Jamie has a condition known as sepsis." "This has happened from bacteria entering in her bloodstream." The bacteria entered her bloodstream because she had a generalized inflammation throughout her body." "The inflammation was caused by a badly infected cut that extends the entire length of her back, from her lower neck area to her buttocks." "At this time, we do not know what caused this, however, there are some other circumstances associated with the cut that law enforcement is anxious to share with you, in case you can shed some light on their inquiries." "More importantly, you need to know Jamie is very sick." "She is in critical condition." "We have isolated the bacteria, and there are three different organisms in the culture." "We have the strongest antibiotics running in her IVs that cover these bacterial strains." "In addition, there is an anti-inflammatory medication running in her IV as well; medication designed to help with the septic state." "She is not responding because she is sedated." "One of the IVs has a sedative running because we want her quiet, and not fighting the ventilator."

Everyone was dabbing their eyes and passing the tissue box from person to person. Ronnie was the first to speak, "how long ago do you think she got this cut?"

"We are estimating around 72 hours." "It is a good thing she was brought in when she was, or I would be giving you much worse news."

"Who brought her in?" Victor asked.

"I actually do not know."

"What are her chances?" Chester said with some clarity.

"Her blood pressure is stable now." "At first we struggled with that." "She was very dehydrated on top of everything else." "The thing we will be watching now will be her kidneys, and her response to the antibiotics, and anti-inflammatory."

Dr. Williams surveyed the group, who looked very distressed. As many times as he had to face grieving families, he still had to show empathy and stay professional during one of these sessions, which at times could be difficult. "What she does have going for her, is she is young and healthy." "Obviously a strong vital young woman before this unfortunate thing happened to her." "Her chances of survival increase for that reason alone." "I do think the circumstances surrounding the cut on her back, maybe precarious at best because as neat and clean as that cut is, it was made with a very sharp object." "It is at least an inch deep." "I urge you to keep this under wraps until you talk to the authorities, and they can advise you from there." "I have probably said more than I should." "The California Sheriff's patrol is waiting to talk with you." "I have asked them to wait until you are composed and ready to answer their questions." Again the Dr. stood to survey the group. No one seemed to want to ask any more questions. He suspected they were overwhelmed, as he would be. "The nurses have my number; if I am not available Miss Rivers will be at your disposal." "If the nursing staff cannot answer your questions; please feel free to have them call me anytime." "I know this is a very difficult time for you, and you have some talking and thinking to do." "I will leave you alone now and ask the charge nurse to be available if you need her." "Also, you can let her know when you want to speak to the officers." "I will be talking with you again in the morning."

Chester stood and again shook the Dr.'s hand, "thank you, Dr. Williams." Victor also stood and shook Dr. Williams hand as he exited the room, with Miss Rivers behind him.

CHAPTER XXV

Green pastures, blue sky, and white fences....is there anything more beautiful? The breeze is so cool. The horses are spirited today, running after one another. Redman isn't a colt anymore, and there he is running with them. "God, I love that big animal." "I will be so glad when I can ride him again."

"I know you will Jamie," Mary said, "It won't be long honey, just be patient."

"Hey, mom lets run along the fence line, like the horses."

"Yes, lets' do, let the wind blow in our hair, and hold hands."

"I love you, mom."

"I love you too Jamie."

"Oh my God.... the lightning....it is raining, the day is ruined." "The train pulled in.... where did that come from?"

"Who is there?" "Who is he?"

"Run child....run ....run....."

"Charles, is that you?"

"Ok, turn her on three; one, two, three." "When you change her dressing, there is an order for ointment."

I can't breathe....I can't talk......Oh God, it hurts.....

"Hit the code button.... NOW, HIT IT!"

"This is such a crazy dream I am having." "Grandfather, Ronnie, standing together.... crying?" "Alex is holding.... Audrey?" "Victoria.... she is hysterical, and Victor.... daddy?" "What the hell is going on?" "That is me.... that is me." "Am I dead?" "It doesn't hurt anymore, but why am I here watching them?" "So, it is over?"

"Not yet, child, it is not over yet."

"Charles?" "Oh, my sweet God, it is you!"

"You can't touch me Jamie, but can ya feel me?"

"Yes, are you alright?" "You look so young and handsome."

"Well, now that's mighty sweet a you child." "But you gotta go back now, you have things to do."

"No, I want to stay with you," "Hey.... Charles where are you." "Please don't leave me again."

"Mr. Blackstone?"

"Yes, Miss Rivers."

"Dr. Williams would like to speak to all of you again." "In the room, we were in before would be fine."

Dr. Williams tried to be swift in his delivery. He felt this family had been through more than they deserved. "As you all know, we had a bit of a downturn in Jamie's condition." "She nearly left us for good." "But since that point, she is dramatically improving, and I do not have an answer as to why, but we will take it."

A scream of joy escaped Victoria's lips, as others embraced and gave thanks. "Perhaps her immune system is finally responding to the antibiotics." "Right now, all systems are looking good, but we will keep her on the critical list for at least 24 hours." "We will start weaning her off the sedative, the ventilator, and hope and pray she keeps responding as she has been recently."

Chester grabbed Dr. William's hand, "I don't know how to thank you for all you have done."

"No need, just being a doctor." "The credit goes to Jamie, who is obviously a tough little nut."

"I do know the authorities have been patiently waiting to talk with all of you." "So, if you don't mind I will turn you over to them." "We will keep you updated on Jamie's condition, and hopefully you can start to see her soon."

"Thank you, doctor, thank you so much," was a universal response from everyone.

The family was still rejoicing when the detectives stepped into the room. After a cordial introduction to everyone, Deputy Sheriff Miranda spoke first, "I am Sheriff Miranda." I will try to start from the beginning, and the detectives will fill in what I might miss." "First of all, this is Detective Sanchez of Morgan County Division and Detective Andrews of the FBI."

"The FBI?" responded Victor.

"Yes Sir, I will explain as we go along." "Miss Blackstone was obviously attacked." "The wound that was made on her back was from a very sharp knife." "It was a straight blade, large like an expensive steel kitchen knife, or a knife like one used for targets." "She had other wounds as well, more like scratches from fingernails, as well as bruises in nearly every area of her body." "Her breast area and inner thigh area are the most evident of a struggle." "Most likely her attacker was attempting to sexually molest and rape her, and she was fighting back."

At this point, the room was void of any sound. Everyone in the room stood like statues made of stone, unbelieving that this could have happened.

"The story begins to get very strange at this point." "We know that at some time Miss Blackstone was staying at a fleabag motel in the downtown area of Richmond." "She stayed at this place for about two weeks." "The local police received a tip that she was hold-up there." "The old lady there is not saying anything, but we think she tipped her off." "Miss Blackstone obviously fled the area." "We do not know how she ended up in Portsmouth." "There is no record of cab or train fare, so she got a ride from someone." "She checked into the Travelers Lodge late Thursday night." "She paid for everything in cash." "The hotel manager stated she called for towels often and refused to let anyone in the room." "She told the maid she would change the bed sheets because they had some blood on them from her menstrual cycle and she was embarrassed about it." "She was apparently sick with the flu, and what room service she called for was hot coffee and soup." "If she left the room at any time, no one saw her." "We believe, however, she was attacked on the night or early morning of her arrival." "No one was seen entering the building after hours, and the cameras did not pick up anything." "The security system is old and outdated, does not work half the time so we are not surprised." "On Saturday night, again early morning hours there was an accident on the train tracks just east of the Travel Lodge." "The man driving the car was one Richard Mongo."

Victoria gasped, and fell back in a chair with her hand over her mouth. Even though, Detective Miranda stopped to observe Victoria's reaction, as did everyone else in the room, he continued on speaking with very little response to her reaction.

"Mr. Mongo is a long time criminal, involved with drug smuggling, prostitution, fraud, theft, as well as murder." "He was a high paid killer, who has been under surveillance for a year by the FBI Drug Task Force, and the local as well as state officials." "We have never been able to make much stick because of the high paid lawyers involved." "He has always been a slippery eel for law enforcement." "No one can figure out what he was doing there, or how he knew where she was." "The facts, however, are beginning to come together." "Even though the train hit the car directly, and it burst into flames, the medical examiner says Mongo actually died at least 36 hours before the wreck." "Dr. Rose Adams stated that Mongo's body composition was strange like he had bled out before driving the car in front of the train." "The most compelling evidence is his DNA was found in the room Miss Blackstone stayed in." "Also, she did not leave until Monday morning." "We have her on tape boarding a 10:00am flight to L.A. "Even though the room was cleaned thoroughly; carpeting, as well as the mattress, there was a large amount of blood on the floor of that room." "There was also a large amount of blood in the drain pipes of the bathtub." "There is evidence that shows a body had been dragged into the bathroom from the bed area."

At this point, Sheriff Miranda nodded to Detective Sanchez, who began speaking slowly, and deliberately, as if it would be difficult for the group to grasp.

"We believe at this point Mr. Mongo was there to kill Ms. Blackstone, as a paid hit."

There was a gasp from among the group. Alex exclaimed, "why, good God, who would do such a thing to someone like Jamie?"

Victoria sat quietly crying, Victor looked pale in obvious disbelief. Chester stood shaking his head, and Audrey leaned against Alex for support. Ronnie, red-faced, jaw clenched, trembling with anger, stood with his hands in his pockets.

"We would like to know the answer to that very question, Mr. Buchanan." "However, we would like to know who killed him." "Someone killed him in that room, moved him to the car, and onto the train tracks to be obliterated." "Pretty hard to believe Jamie did all that by herself, in self-defense." "It is almost physically impossible for a young girl to have accomplished that feat." "By the time he was hit by the train, significant rigors had set in, and quite frankly I am not sure I could have done it." "We think someone came to her aid, defended her, and then helped her get rid of the body." "What is strange is there is absolutely not one tiny bit of evidence as to who that could have been."

"If this was anyone who gave a damn about her, how could they have left her there?" "Who would do such a thing?" Yelled an exasperated furious Ronnie. His eyes filled with angry tears, as he walked to the window to stare out into the distance. "She said this; she always believed someone had killed her mother and Charles." "Oh my God, she said she was going to find out who!" "I…. never thought…." Now Ronnie's emotions were unrestrained, and he left the room unable to control his anger or tears.

"Detective Andrews does have more to add," said Detective Sanchez.

Unlike Sheriff Miranda and Detective Sanchez, Detective Andrews was a woman. A small blond woman, with an athletic build, and poker face; not one indication in her demeanor of any emotion she might be feeling.

"We do know that Jamie met with Mongo approximately 30 days ago." "We also know her grandmother had met with him separately directly before this, and it is believed the grandmother had no knowledge of Jamie's meeting with him."

Chester's red-rimmed eyes opened wide, mouth agape, "What?" "How do you know this?"

"Mr. Mongo has been under surveillance for drug trafficking, so their presence turned up on the tape."

By this time Ronnie had returned to the room and was standing quietly behind everyone, listening.

Victoria had not quit sobbing and finally said, "I knew, God I knew she had seen him." "This is my fault." "She begged me not to say anything and I didn't.... I didn't."

"But why, why would she meet with him," asked Audrey?

Ronnie answered for Victoria, "because she believed Sophia had her mother killed, and Charles too."

"Yes, that is right!" exclaimed Victoria.

Chester sat down hard on the nearest chair, still shaking his head back and forth, rubbing his chest.

Detective Andrews walked to Chester, "are you, alright sir?"

Everyone was now looking at Chester, he wasn't talking; he had grown extremely pale, and was sweating profusely. Alex hurriedly walked to the nurse's station to get help. In seconds three nurses appeared with aspirin and sublingual nitroglycerin. Shortly after Dr. Williams arrived.

CHAPTER XXVI

Emptiness is a void or a vacuum. When an individual feels an emptiness, there is a lack of meaning or purpose; there are numbness and despair. As Jamie sat gazing at the ocean repeating the same motion of ebb tides, she could only feel hollowness. She wanted nothing; no food, water, or connection to another human. She felt betrayed by humanity and certainly by God; which she no longer believed in. She pretended to remember nothing; not how she ran away from the ranch, the attack by Mongo, his death, or how she ended up in California. She used her trauma to avoid questions from authorities, family, and friends. She would stare at them blankly but harboring one emotion which enveloped her every waking moment, and that continued to be the rage.

The physicians helped her by defending her behavior, then defining what trauma can do to the human mind. They explained away her behavior because of the attack, her injury and, the unfortunate death of loved ones, all a reason for her inability to remember the past weeks. She obviously was in shock and maybe her memory would return someday. Chester's death was the final blow. He had suffered a massive heart attack at the hospital, rushed to emergency cardiac intervention, but to no avail. He died before Jamie was discharged from the hospital. Jamie was unable to attend his funeral.

The police and FBI were at a total standstill in their investigation. No one could come up with a scenario of how Mongo could have ended up on the train tracks, there was no evidence of a second person helping Jamie. The authorities were convinced Jamie could not have done this alone, and Jamie appeared to remember nothing. Sophia denied any association with Mongo even after being shown the surveillance tapes she said he just happened to be sitting at her table because he knew the owner of the establishment she was dining at. She merely was making room for a young man who needed a place to sit while waiting for a woman. No one could dispute this, no one could prove Sophia had any involvement with a known killer.

Sophia now wealthier than ever had no one, only the servants she paid to help her. She was being questioned by police, shunned by friends, and ignored by her only son, who she felt should be at her side through this most difficult time. Instead, he was with who she hated most, Jamie. Sophia kept replaying her known association with Mongo. Theodore would not say a word about how or why she came to know him, or it would implicate Theodore himself. She did not ask that greasy frightening man to kill Jamie. She just wanted her to go away; to scare her away. The idea that she would hire a reprehensible man like that to kill anyone was ridiculous. After all, she was just taking the advice of her dear friend Theodore, who now refused to even see or talk to her. She just had no one.

The old black man was nothing more than an ignorant roach and she had counted on his death making Jamie more vulnerable. With each day she spent in solitude, she grew more withdrawn and vengeful. How could a woman like her end up like this? She wanted to fly to Germany, and perhaps set up residence near some distant family members. She needed to escape this horrible life and all who had turned their backs on her. Yes, even her precious

Victor, who stood vigil for Jamie but cared nothing for his own mother. The authorities had informed her she could not leave the State of Virginia until the investigation into Mongo's death was closed. How insulting and degrading. She did not deserve this. She was selling off those horses, and anything else that was an animal on this stinking ranch she despised. She officially fired Ronnie the day after Chester's funeral, "good riddance," she would say under her breath. She could not sell the ranch or Jamie's horse because part of the ownership was left in Jamie's name, unbeknown to her, Chester's own wife. She had no one to talk to, except that strange little man, the driver Morrie. He talked to her and seemed interested in her welfare. He was a strange looking man, but a little gentleman did not speak unless spoken to, was kind, and respectful of her. Maybe she would at least talk to him a bit more. What did she have to lose at this point? She was suffocating here and the rumination she continued with her every waking moment was destroying her and she could feel it. There had to be a way out.

Jamie stayed with Audrey in CA. She did not want to go near the ranch but did ask on a regular basis where Redman was and if he could be transported to CA. She was told by Sophia's lawyer through her own representative that Redman would remain on the ranch until the estate was settled and apparently that would not be until they closed the case on Mongo.

Victoria finally returned to Virginia with her parents so she could finish school. She called frequently, but often Jamie refused to take any calls.

Ronnie returned to Wyoming to his ranch for the time being. Since Jamie refused to talk to him, or see him it seemed futile to remain in CA. He would return if she needed him, but he intended to start his own investigation of all that had transpired, since Jamie's mother's death. He had to know himself what had happened and at times thought of nothing else. Who helped Jamie? Why was Mongo in that room? Why did Sophia officially fire him when she knew he was gone from the property? Even though he knew Sophia hated Jamie none of this made sense. Now he had lost his best friend Chester. A man who believed in him supported him, and even in anger was there for him.

Mary had the baby, a boy. A part of him wanted to see his son, another part wanted nothing to do with Mary. He would take one day at a time, but first, spend some time with his aging parents, then a trip to Gray Mountain.

CHAPTER XXVII

"From Proverbs 6:16-19, there are six things that the Lord hates, seven that are an abomination to him: haughty eyes, and a lying tongue, hands that shed innocent blood, a heart that devises wicked plans, feet that make haste to run to evil, a false witness who breathes out lies, and one who sows discord among brothers." "Jamie…. Jamie, are you listening to any of these readings?" Father Albright was visiting Jamie at Audrey's request. He would always end his visit by reading to her from the Bible. Today he appeared overly concerned with her attention span. Jamie did not mind his visits, she just did not listen to him. Her mind would dwell in another world as he babbled on and on about forgiveness and lately a good deal of the subject matter was about what hate would do to one's soul. He was a kind old man with sad eyes, and what appeared on the surface to be a pure heart. Out of respect for Audrey, and in an effort to keep her world private, she would remain quiet and somewhat despondent.

"I hear you, sir," Jamie responded.

"Do you understand what the passage is saying?" Father Albright said urging her response.

"Yes, I understand Father."

"Well, then I think we will continue on at another time." "You seem a bit tired today Jamie; maybe you would like to rest?"

"Yes, sir."

Jamie could hear Father Albright talking with Audrey by the front door. He was worried about her despondency, and lack of interest. Just gathering what she could hear, it sounded like he was recommending a professional, a psychiatrist for Jamie in the future who could perhaps prescribe medication for severe depression. It was definitely time to move ahead with plans.

The rap on the door startled her, and Audrey was thinking it might be Father Albright that may have forgotten something. It was Victor and his arms were full of sacks filled with groceries. "Hi…I am cooking dinner." "We are having Coq Au Vin." Audrey and Jamie both just stared back in disbelief. "What, you didn't know I could cook?" "Well we are starting with a nice Pinot, and everyone will relax and enjoy."

"Victor, we are so grateful for this and happy to see you," Audrey exclaimed. Jamie stood and then ran to him putting her arms around his neck and weeping softly. Audrey gently took the groceries from Victor as he stood holding Jamie in his arms until she began to calm and the crying stopped.

"Come on baby, you can help me make this wonderful food," Victor said softly to Jamie. Audrey poured the wine and the cooking began with the searing of chicken thighs and legs, then the creation of a creamy wine sauce with mushrooms and the marrying of those ingredients with special seasoning to bake and create a delicious entrée. "You Jamie, my sweet are in charge of the salad and lovely Audrey the potatoes and dessert." "I purchased lemon gelato we can have with fresh berries?" "Is everyone in agreement with the menu I created?"

Victor, the charming, handsome, sober host kept the ladies delightfully entertained. It was the first joyous time Jamie could remember since she came home from the hospital. For the first time in so long, she could barely remember the last time she felt so warm and loved. The evening was glorious because no one mentioned the horrific events that had occurred. There were no questions, or insinuations, just delicious food and good wine that seemed to weave together past feelings of family, like putting Humpty Dumpty's shell back together.

"Daddy, are you getting ready to leave?" said Jaime meekly.

"Yes, I am going back to the hotel." "I have an early flight back to Virginia; still more legal things to take care of with the estate." "Sophia is anxious to sell the ranch and......

"I am going to see her dead."

"What did you say?" Victor said flabbergasted.

"I said, I am going to see her dead," Jamie said sternly.

"Look, honey, the investigation is still continuing and I know how you feel about Sophia, but you need....

"How could you possibly know how I feel?" Jamie responded angrily

"I thought you couldn't remember anything Jamie," Victor exclaimed.

"I.... I can't remember.... much...I just...." Jamie's voice trailed off.

"Jamie, please just rest and let the investigation finish out, and if you remember anything about what took place, please just call me and I will come back here." "I know you miss your horse, which I am glad you remember."

"Please don't let her get rid of my horse Redman, please...please." Jamie wailed.

"I won't, I promise I won't." "It's ok honey, I won't." "Now, give me a big hug, and you go get some sleep." "I love you, and I will call you next week."

"Have you heard from Ronnie?" Jamie asked

"No, no I haven't."

"Alex?"

"No."

CHAPTER XXVIII

After several quiet days on the California coast, Jamie began to settle into a calm reserve. She spent her time planning her every move. She would avenge her mother, Charles, and Chester. She would have peace in this life if it killed her, and right now she had no regard for her own life, except she must survive to complete her plan; then who cared? Everyone would return to their lives; maybe they would occasionally think of her and feel bad that she was gone, but as time passed it would be less and less. She would not be punished for this, not for ridding the world of more garbage. She would die first, that was a solemn promise to herself.

The sound of the ocean waves and her deep thought drown out the sound of the voice. When she first felt hands on her shoulders she reeled around and fell backward onto the wet sand.

"Well now, the last time I had you in the wet sand you were smiling." Looking up into the handsome dark face of Alex she jumped to her feet and embraced him as earnestly as she could. They stood holding each other as minutes passed, neither wanting to let go.

"Oh Alex, I love you, I love you." "Don't let go, just don't let me go," whispered Jamie.

"Awwww, I really wished you meant that in the real sense." Alex softly said brushing the hair from her eyes.

"Will you kiss me?" "I mean really kiss me like you used to when you wanted me, not like I am going to break, or I am your little sister." Alex gently lifted her chin up towards his face and kissed her lips softly and passionately. The kiss lasted long enough that she began to feel heat surging through her body. She felt alive again, really alive. He tasted good and smelled even better. She pressed herself against him, running her hands down his strong muscular back and his firm buttocks.

"Whoa…whoa…. Jamie, slow down my darling." "Let's not get carried away here, you are going to have me repeating our last encounter on the beach."

"Good, do it, make love to me like you did then, I need you, Alex." "Don't you want me anymore?" "Am I too tarnished for you now?" She pleaded.

"Are you kidding?" "Jamie, this is not just sex." "I love you more than that and you know it, so where is this coming from?" "Do you understand what I am saying?"

"Yes, I understand, but where have you been all this time?"

"I have been working." "I was by your side in the hospital, don't you remember?" "I was there when you were discharged, and when they told you about Chester." "You seemed so pitiful and distant; I just thought it might be better if I left you alone for a while to receive help from professionals." "I thought that is what you wanted."

"I don't remember leaving the hospital." "Do you think I am brain damaged or something?" "I heard and saw my mother….and Charles…and me…I saw me…and I was dead." "Oh God, I was dead…I was dead." Tears were running down her face as she repeated the fact that she saw herself being treated by the doctors and nurses. They sat on the beach and Alex continued to hold her until the sunset. She told him the dream she had and how Mary was with her, and Charles warning her, telling her to run. Audrey watched them from the deck and prayed this would help Jamie come back from the dark place she was dwelling in.

Alex stayed the remainder of the week. He even attended her sessions with Father Albright. She felt like she was complete as long as he was near her. She felt happiness as they talked and laughed and shared nearly every minute together. But she had no choice, she must complete her promise, her plan must be done, it would be finished.

CHAPTER XXIX

Ephesians 4:26-27 Be not angry and do not sin; do not let the sun go down on your anger and give no opportunity to the devil.

Matthew 6:14-15 For if you forgive others their trespasses, your heavenly Father will also forgive you, but if you do not forgive others their trespasses, neither will your Father forgive your trespasses.

Ephesians 4:32 Be kind to one another, be tenderhearted, forgiving one another, as God in Christ forgave you.

Proverbs 24:17 Do not rejoice when your enemy falls and let not your heart be glad when he stumbles....

"Jesus Christ!!!!" "Am I losing my mind?" "Father Albright has completely turned my brain into mush!" Jamie screamed to herself as she held her head in her hands. "This crap that he reads me every day...." "God, just give me a break!"

Take away from me the noise of your songs. I will not listen to the music of your harps.

"The noise…the noise…the damn NOISE.!" Jamie screeched still holding her head. But no one was hearing or listening. She could not be heard over the ocean waves. She felt herself descending into blackness, like a tar pit in the middle of her soul. An abyss, a void with nothing but these voices in her head; one repeating what she must do to avenge all that she loved, and had been ripped from her; the other constantly contradicting her need for vengeance. She felt insanity enveloping her from all directions. In addition, she felt a loneliness that suffocated her. No one cared about her pain, no one understood her pain. It was like they were outside the space she was locked in peering through a window, but unable to open it or enter.

She had to get out of here. She had to find a way out of here. If I cannot think I cannot make a plan that will work. "I have to write things down; make a formulated concrete plan or I will be caught before I can complete it. How am I going to escape with these people watching my every move?"

Jamie began to write down a map; an algorithm that only she understood and reviewed it daily. Her every step was planned. She began to feel invigorated with a hope that she would succeed. Audrey and Father Albright were pleased with her sudden change, which is exactly what she hoped for. He gave her copies of passages from the Bible which he was sure was affecting her change. However, she would walk to the ocean's edge and rip them to shreds watching them as they withered in the water and eventually carried out to sea to disintegrate.

Even Alex was impressed on his next visit, but something did seem amiss. He sensed that this might be a front of some sort, that she was just playing a game. "Jamie my love, what is going on with you?"

"Nothing Alex, what is your problem?"

"I don't have a problem but I think you might."

"Why, because I feel better each day?" "Because I am feeling anything at all these days." I would think you would be pleased."

"I am if it is real."

"What is that supposed to mean?" "Are you accusing me of faking a recovery?"

Alex did not answer but continued to gaze deeply into her eyes.

Jamie pulled herself onto his lap straddling him. "Touch me." "Be the man you used to be."

"I am the man I have always been, but maybe I have a little different perspective since I sat by you while you were fighting for your life." "Maybe I actually care more for you then you do for yourself!" Clearly, an irritated Alex appeared to be growing unusually frustrated.

"No, no baby, don't be mad at me." "It's just that I feel empty and lonely." "I need to feel another human close to me." "I need to feel you on top of me, inside me…. I want to feel alive again." "Please help me feel that again, Alex please."

At first, he just kissed her gently, then harder biting her lip. He stood pulling her to her feet and dragging her toward the pier. They went under the pier in a covered place. He again sat on the sand pulling her on top of him. He exposed himself and placed her straddling him entering her as she cried out. He felt amazing, full and swollen undulating inside her. She pulled his shirt apart running her nails down his chest, kissing and sucking on his face and neck. The climax was quick for both, and after it had passed they held each other in the same position.

"Get up," Alex said a little too sternly.

"What?"

"You heard me, let me up."

Jamie rolled to the side as Alex rose to his feet zipping up his pants. He looked very disturbed. "What is wrong Alex?"

"I feel sick."

"Why, did I do something wrong?" "Are you really sick…. are you going to be sick?"

"Yeah, maybe." "This whole thing is horrible and I am ashamed of myself." "Don't you get it?" "Huh, don't you get it?" His voice was growing louder against the crashing ocean waves.

"What is wrong with you Alex?" "It was so satisfying, what I needed…you felt great!" Jamie yelled back at Alex.

"I am not your fuck buddy Jamie, I love you…I always have; this is wrong, it's wrong!"

Jamie was shocked at his passion and anger. His voice cracked and trembled with emotion as he turned to leave. Jamie yelled at him "wait, please just wait." But to no avail, Alex then broke into a run leaving hurriedly in his car.

Jamie was in awe of what just happened. She could not fathom what he meant, running the event over and over in her mind. This was so unlike Alex. She returned to her room to go over her plan. No matter how hard she tried she could not get Alex's words or expressions from her mind.

Did he really love her as a woman, not a close friend, not like a brother, but as a couple? Did she think of him like that? Could he take the place of Ronnie in her heart? Why not? Where the hell was Ronnie? Where had he been? It did not matter. What mattered was completing the plan. She knew if she was going to finish this, that all of her life before would need to end anyway. What did it matter if Alex or anyone loved her or not; it was going to be finished.

CHAPTER XXX

The following weeks were quiet and repetitive. Jamie asked Audrey to take her shopping on several occasions. Each time as she bought meaningless things, she also purchased something of value that would help her with her plan but Audrey would not understand.

She had not heard anything from Alex. She tried to call him once but hung up after the first ring. "It would only hurt him more," she whispered softly to herself. Victor had called once to check on her, telling her he was flying to Texas on company business and would return in a week or so. He would call when he returned. Now is the time.

Audrey was busy making sandwiches when Jamie returned from her walk by the ocean. Jamie looked closely at her. She appeared tired, with dark circles under her eyes, and aging lines around her mouth. She seemed so sad to Jamie and it occurred to her she had been so busy with her own thoughts that she had failed to notice Audrey's appearance. "I am so sorry aunt, Audrey," as she wrapped her arms around

Audrey's shoulders, hugging her tightly. "I have been such a drain on you, and I can be so selfish." "You are a wonderful person and I might not have recovered if it had not been for you." "I do love you." Audrey began to softly cry. "Oh, I am so sorry I am such a burden on you."

"Jamie... Jamie, please you are not a burden." "I have just been so worried about you." "I guess a part of me wishes Ralph could be here to help and encourage both of us." "I miss him."

"I know you do sweetheart." "Me being here has not let you get on with your life." "Promise me you will now do that; get on with life." "Ok?"

"Yes Jamie, now that you are doing so much better, I will get on with it," Audrey stated in an animated whimsical manner. "Let's please eat, I am starving." With giggles and more hugs, they then sat down for lunch.

"Victoria, is that you?"

"Jamie?"

"Yes, my little friend it is Jamie."

"Oh my God," Victoria exclaimed. "Are you ok?" "You sound wonderful." "When can I come and see you?"

"Soon honey, soon." "I just wanted to talk to you for a little bit and let you know I am sorry I did not take all your phone calls." "It has been hard coming back from a dark place and I did not want to talk for a long time." "I hope you can understand; you have always been like a little sister and I love you."

There was a long silence and then Victoria responded in a weak voice, "I love you too…are you sure you are ok?"

"Never better." "Now tell me, what have you been up to." "Fill me in because talking about me is depressing." "I want to hear something positive, and maybe nasty," both laughing at this. The remainder of their conversation was of Victoria's happenings. All the while Victoria felt an uneasiness that she could not explain. They parted with promises to see each other soon and make plans on their lives ahead as sisters.

CHAPTER XXXI

The morning air was cold and the water freezing. The wet-suit and life jacket had made a difference but she still shivered uncontrollably as she made her way toward the land that jutted out into the ocean. She was running again, but this time had no intention of getting caught by anyone especially by a murdering psychopath. The supplies she had packed were in a flotation device that made it easy to pull beside her. The hardest thing was crawling up the embankment and pulling the supplies up behind her. She lay down on the rocky edge to rest before unpacking the items that would be her only belongings for a long period of time. The walk to the bus-stop seemed endless. After struggling with the supplies, burying what she did not need on her journey, and walking with this backpack for three miles, she could feel the fatigue washing over her. She had not eaten before embarking and she now regretted that. She was shaking but she could not stop for fear of not reaching the bus-stop in time.

Old Sam the bus driver smiled widely when seeing Jamie. "Well good afternoon young lady." "Where you off to?"

"Hi Sam, I am going to town and catch the train to San Francisco." "Gonna go visit a friend." "You doing good Sam?"

"Yes, I am my dear," Sam said continuing to smile.

"Sam, can I ask a favor of you?"

"Of course."

"When you go home, would you mind dropping this off in Aunt Audrey's mailbox?" "I forgot to leave this for her with directions on where I will be staying." Jamie handed Joe a small envelope that contained a letter telling Audrey to understand why she must go and ask for forgiveness for making her worry. It also said it would be futile to look for her and to please not try.

"I don't mind at all, but you know it will be about 6:00pm after I am shut down for the evening."

"Yes, I know, and that is fine, she won't be home till after that."

Jamie thought, "seems like I tell more lies than truths these days," She knew Sam lived just down the road from Audrey. She knew his schedule well and that Audrey and Sam had been friends for years. Audrey was going to be home but would not start looking for Jamie until after dinner, thinking she was just out walking again, or maybe had taken the bus to town to buy something. Jamie had purposely taken the bus to town often lately so Audrey would get used to her being away for extended periods.

Jamie spent the time swimming to the island knowing she must rid herself of some supplies and buying herself time. She often awoke early and walked by the ocean before Audrey got up, so that would not be unusual. This morning for Jamie the day had started at 5:00am and walking into the dark ocean waves took some courage but was necessary.

Reaching town Jamie went into the train depot long enough for Sam to pull away from the bus stop. She then walked to a truck-stop a few blocks away. Jamie was ravenous and ordered a chicken dinner and cola. She was also listening intently to some of the conversation going on between the truckers in the next booth. One in particular interested her. For one thing, he was a little more respectful with his language knowing a female was nearby. He talked about his wife in Florida and how he was anxious to "see her and his parents." Perfect....

Jamie watched him as he left and she followed. As he walked up to the semi-truck he was driving, she startled him as she touched his shoulder. "Sir, could I ride with you?" He stared at her incredulously.

"Look, mam, I do not want a prostitute."

Jamie chuckled a little, "believe me I don't want that either." "I just need a ride." "I will pay you."

He hesitated long enough to make her nervous. "Never mind, I will try someone else."

"Wait, you look pretty young, you running away?"

Jamie was shaking again. "I am twenty-two, and yes I am running from a man who thinks it is ok to beat me up." "I need to get somewhere close to Florida and then I can call some cousins that will come and get me."

Again, he hesitated as seconds passed. "Why don't you just take a plane or a bus?"

"Because he will follow me."

"Have you called the police and told them?" He looked concerned.

"Many times, but they cannot always be there." Jamie tried to look like she was near tears.

He looked down shaking his head and muttering "shit." "You know we are at least three days out of Florida." "I mean you are not sleeping with me."

"That's ok, I can pay for a room if you will just park in the lot." "Or I have a sleeping bag and I do not mind sleeping on the seat." "I can pay you, would you take $1000?"

"A thousand dollars…. you can pay me a thousand dollars?" He said obviously surprised.

"I will give you half now," Jamie responded.

"This better not be illegal." "I do not need any trouble."

"You won't have any, I promise," Jamie responded earnestly.

"Alright, get in."

"What is your name?"

"My name is Arthur; people just call me Art." "Yours?"

"Rhonda."

"Ok Rhonda, I don't talk much."

"Good, me either."

CHAPTER XXXII

The response to Jamie's departure was swift and more reactionary then Jamie may have anticipated. There was an all-points bulletin issued for her by the next afternoon.

With Mongo's case open and interest still shown by the State. the FBI, and local authorities, the report of Jamie's disappearance was immediate. Jamie knew this because of a report on the TV in a local truck stop in Tucson, AZ.

She thought about running at that very moment but thought better of it deciding to take a chance on Art's anti-social side. He talked very little, listened to some classical music, did not like television, and read a book when they stopped to rest. He was a strange type to be a truck driver, and Jamie thought to herself on more than one occasion, he has to be running from something himself. She purchased a hooded sweatshirt at one of the stops and made sure to have the hood up whenever they stopped to rest or purchase food.

Once again many of the same people had come together to discuss Jamie's disappearance. An angry and frustrated Ronnie, a bewildered Audrey, a regretful saddened Victor and a very remorseful Alex; with authorities discussing how could this girl so skillfully vanish again? The only reason they did not question foul play was old Sam's response to authorities on Jamie's ride into town. The letter Sam had delivered to Audrey was not found stuck in the front entrance until the following morning. It was full of apologies about the abruptness of Jamie's departure and asking Audrey to forgive her for her decision to leave, stating she needed to be completely alone.

Victor was the most vocal repeating over and over, "how could this happen again?" Ronnie and Alex stood on opposite sides of the room occasionally glaring at each other. It was Ronnie who made the first move. "So, did she say anything to you that might lead to where she might be?"

Alex turned to see who was saying that to him. He was irritated to see Ronnie standing behind him. He could feel his face flush with anger. "Don't you think if I knew anything I would speak up?"

Ronnie stepped back slightly, "maybe I said that wrong." "I apologize." "You have spent some time with her, and I just thought…." his voice fading.

"Look," Alex continued with deliberate slowness, "I have been racking my brain trying to remember everything she said in the last few days I saw her." "I am worried because she kept talking about dreams about her mother and Charles." "She said she felt like she was losing her mind, and that she was really lonely." "Our last meeting wasn't so good." "I mean I was frustrated and angry; I just walked away." "I wish I could undo that."

Ronnie stood looking at Alex who was obviously in pain. For the first time, he realized he was looking at someone who loved Jamie as much as he did and may deserve her more. "You don't think she would hurt herself, do you?" "You are scaring the shit out of me."

"I know," Alex said softly

"What should we do?" Ronnie was earnestly asking for an answer.

"I don't know Ron," Alex shaking his head, "I just don't know."

"Christ."

The trip seemed to go on and on. "How does anyone do this for a living?" Jamie thought to herself. Art was just not opening up to any discussions. He treated her like she was not there. She kept thinking, "this is best," "no attachments, no connection at all." However, the need for the human attachment poured over her and when that happened, she would close her eyes and pretend to sleep, dreaming of the past when life was happy and carefree. "Art can you stop at the next truck stop?" "I need a bathroom break."

"Yeah, I could use a break myself."

Tallahassee, Florida was the place and Jamie could hardly wait to put her feet on the ground again. She took her time, washing her face, brushing her teeth, and spending more time than usual brushing her hair. As she walked out of the bathroom to find where Art was, her heart nearly stopped. He stood in front of a TV watching the news, and starring at the face of the missing girl, Jamie Blackstone. She quickly pulled up the hood on her jacket and walked up beside him. "If you will just let me get my things out of your truck I will disappear."

"Looks like you are pretty good at that." He waited a few moments then quietly whispered, "Jacksonville is about 150 miles from here." "I will drop you off there and you go wherever you are going and forget you ever met me." "Is that a deal?"

"Yes sir," Jamie said thankfully.

The ride to Jacksonville was made without a word uttered between Art and Jamie. When they stopped it was near an airport shuttle booth. "This is where you get off." Jamie quietly gathered her belongings and stepped down out of the truck. "The ticket area is over there, and the taxi area is behind the entrance, just follow the signs to what you want," as he pointed off in the distance. Jamie stood outside the truck door gazing up at him. Then he said something shocking. "I knew your grandfather." "He was a good man." "I hope you figure this out." "Do what he would have wanted you to do." With that, he pulled the door shut and left, Jamie standing and staring after him, as the shuttle pulled up.

Jamie didn't take the shuttle. She sat on the bench just inside the covered area for an undetermined amount of time. People were stopping and going from the area, but Jamie could not have recalled what anyone looked like. One gray-haired gentleman stopped to offer her a piece of chewing gum, asking if she was alright. She nodded her head but paid no attention to him. She felt nothing. She did not feel pain or anger. Even the rage and yearning for revenge seemed to ebb like the ocean tide. Art's face and his words, "I knew your grandfather," would not leave her thoughts. She walked to the beach and stopped at a sign that said *Yacht Club*. The sun was setting and it would be dark soon. She cut through a golfing range and ended up at a storage building adjacent to the property. It was unlocked and, in the back, there was an office with a couch, desk, and chairs. Jamie lay down on the couch and fell asleep.

Voices woke her in the early morning. She sat up and her heart was pounding hard, she grabbed her backpack and hurried to the office door. She hid behind some stacked up boxes just outside the office and waited for the voices to subside. She saw a man walking into the office and sitting at the desk. She waited until she thought her bladder might burst. She had to do something and now. She began to crawl on the floor slowly to a place past the window of the office where the man at the desk could not see her. At that point, she raced down the hall and out the open door nearly knocking over a gardener. "Hey, where you going?" he shouted. She kept running as fast as she could until she could not run anymore. She stopped near a gas station and entered the restroom. She looked at herself in the mirror and was sickened by the vision she was looking at. She was very pale and tired looking. She was ravenous and filthy with visible dirt on her face and clothing. Jamie washed her face with the hand soap in the dispenser and changed into the only other set of clothes she had that were worn but not stained with dirt. She took out a purse that contained all the money she brought with her. She brushed her teeth and braided her hair.

The new image was a definite improvement. She walked into the combination gas station, restaurant, and convenience store. She walked up to the counter and spoke to the young man busily cooking on a grill. "Hi, whatever you are cooking smells really good."

"I am making burritos." "You want one?" He said smiling.

"Yes, I would love one."

"Bacon or sausage?"

"Just egg and cheese, no meat."

"Some peppers and onions ok?"

"Yes, that is fine and I want some orange juice."

Jamie sat at a small table out in front of the convenience store. The morning air felt good and the burrito tasted like the best thing she had ever put in her mouth. She went back for a second burrito and coffee. "Man, you eat a lot for a girl."

"Yes, well I am hungry."

After leaving the store Jamie walked to the edge of Jacksonville and purchased a car. A small decent looking used car. It was an expenditure that she did not plan for but was necessary. It took her cash funds to a low level, but she knew where she could get more when she needed it without too many questions. The cash purchase was easy and a simple signing over of the title. The man was a seedy looking fast talker but did not argue with the cash or ask questions. She would need to be very careful driving along the highways; being stopped at this point would be the end of the road for her. She also purchased a hat, sunglasses, and a large beach bag that would take the place of the backpack.

The destination was a hotel just outside of Richmond. Unlike other places, Jamie had stayed when on the run, this hotel was five stars. It was an attractive brick structure with an arched entrance and various shops, restaurants, bistros and a spa on the first floor. The valet parking for her was perfect; the car tucked away in a safe place with little scrutiny. The only hitch was during check-in. The gentleman insisted on a major credit card, stating the policy of the hotel was not to take cash for payment. It took a conversation with the manager and another lie of a lost purse with all her credit cards gone and stating she would leave for another hotel if they refused to take her payment, the manager agreed to allow her to pay for a two-day stay. After a long hot shower and room service, she collapsed on the bed for a much-needed sleep.

Instead of sleep, every time she began to drift off she would remember Mongo and wake up with a jolt at which time she would again get up and check the lock on the door. This room reminded her too much of the night of the attack.

As soon as the shops opened for business in the morning Jamie called down to the hair salon on the first floor for an appointment. "I want it cut short and dyed black." Jamie showed the stylist from a magazine what she wanted to be done with her hair.

"I am not going to argue with you, but you have beautiful hair," the stylist pleaded. "Are you sure you want to make this drastic change?"

"Yes, that is what I want." "I want a change." Jamie also purchased make-up, a dress, and a black suit and shoes. The next morning when Jamie gazed at herself in the mirror she was impressed with the change. She achieved exactly the look she wanted. She looked at least five years older than she was. Dressed in her black suit and heels she looked sophisticated and classy. Jamie called the front desk, "Could you please call me a taxi for a 2:00pm pick-up?"

CHAPTER XXXIII

"Good morning, how may I help you?" Morrie stood staring at a man and woman dressed in a suit and tie at the front door of the Blackstone mansion.

"Good afternoon sir, I am Detective Mayes of the Richmond police department and this is Detective Andrews of the FBI." "We would like to speak to Mrs. Blackstone." "I believe she was expecting us."

"Yes sir, please come in," Morrie stepped back motioning for the detectives to enter. He led the detectives into the parlor off the dining area. "May I have Lydia serve you some coffee and refreshments?"

"That is very nice of you but really not necessary, we do not plan to be here long."

"Well detectives, it is too late, she has already prepared it so you can partake of what you like." With that Morrie hobbled to the kitchen announcing on his way "I will let Ms. Sophia Blackstone know that you are here and ready to speak with her."

"Actually Mr....hum...what did you say your full name was?" "Mr. Morrie...?" Detective Mayes was waiting for an answer from Morrie.

"Lewis sir. My name is William Morrison Lewis sir." "Everyone calls me Morrie...sir."

"I see, well Morrie we would like to speak to you as well." "We can talk with you now before you fetch Mrs. Blackstone, or we can speak with you after." "What would work for you, Morrie?"

"Now is fine sir." Morrie stiffly sat down with the help of this cane in a chair across from the two detectives.

"Well good, let us get on with it then." They paused for a short while as Lydia, one of the new cooks served coffee and some freshly baked sugar cookies.

"Morrie, we are assuming that you know Jamie Blackstone."

"Yes sir, I do."

"You know Morrie, we interviewed everyone in that school Jamie attended, about the day she disappeared from the ranch, and somehow made it to downtown Richmond. One of the janitors at the school she attended, a Mister Drisdol, I believe, described you as the one who dropped her at the school." "Is that true?" "Did you drop her off at the school that day?"

Morrie answered slowly, "Yes, I did drop her there."

"Why is it we are just now hearing this, Morrie?" "Why hadn't you told anyone, particularly her grandfather who even had rewards offered for information leading to locating her, that you dropped her at the school?"

"Because sir, she asked me not to say anything."

"Excuse me, Mr. Lewis, Mr. Blackstone was your employer, and you had to know he was worried about the disappearance of his granddaughter, and you saw fit to say nothing?" "Why is that?"

Again, Morrie took his time answering. "She asked me not to say anything." "She seemed frightened and I thought after the drama subsided she would return from the school."

Detective Andrews seemed incredulous at Morrie's obvious vagueness. "And when she didn't return you said nothing?"

"Yes, sir."

"Why?" Both detectives responded simultaneously still trying to comprehend his answer.

"Because she seemed afraid, and I did not want any trouble."

"Does Mrs. Blackstone know about this?"

"No, sir."

It was obvious they were going to get nowhere with Morrie at this point.

"Alright Morrie, would you please get Mrs. Blackstone now?"

As Morrie struggled to get up with his cane, detective Mayes rose to assist him. Morrie then proceeded to the kitchen to call Sophia from the house phone.

"What the hell was all that about?" Detective Andrews said, to detective Mayes.

"I have no idea, but he is damn strange."

Minutes passed before Sophia finally entered the parlor. Both stood when she approached. Detective Andrews held out her hand to greet her, which Sophia ignored and sat down in the chair across from the detectives.

"What can I help you officers with?"

"We are not sure if you have heard but Jamie Blackstone is missing again." "Have you seen or heard from her?"

"Sophia let out a big sigh "when are you people going to figure out that child is crazy?" "Well, not a child any longer, but a full-grown adult who has nearly destroyed my family and my life." "She keeps this charade of poor little me up for everyone when in reality she is insane."

Detective Andrews, disgusted responded with, "Mrs. Blackstone isn't Jamie Blackstone your paternal granddaughter?" "Aren't you the least bit concerned with her safety or health?"

"Listen to me young woman, this girl is a demon." "She was born to a woman who trapped my son with a pregnancy." "I opened my home to her after that witch died, and she has done nothing but bring evil, and destruction down on my head." Sophia began to screech hysterically, "my son is gone, my husband is dead, my servants left, and I have been accused of trying to kill her." "Why should I be concerned?" "I hope she is dead." Sophia then crying and sobbing into a tissue that Morrie had brought to her during her tirade.

The detectives sat quietly watching her closely. "Why are you sitting there staring at me?" "Why are you here?" "Do I need to call my lawyer before I say anything else?" "Are you planning on charging me with something?"

With that, the detectives stood up and Detective Mayes stated, "actually that won't be necessary Mrs. Blackstone, you are not charged with anything." "We just wanted to make you aware we do not know where Jamie is either."

"So, do I need protection?" Sophia screeched.

"Do you think you need protection?" Detective Andrews asked with a deliberate slow steady enunciation.

Sophia was quiet for a moment contemplating her answer, "No, I do not need or want protection." She then dropped her head wiping her eyes.

"We will be leaving then." Detective Mayes nodded to Morrie as they both headed for the front entrance.

"She is one creepy old woman." Detective Mayes uttered.

"Yeah, she is." "They both are." "This whole damn situation is."

CHAPTER XXXIV

The United States went to war in Vietnam in 1965 believing that the war would be quickly over with this small underdeveloped country facing the might of American forces. President Lyndon Baines Johnson wanted nothing more than the confrontation to end quickly so he could proceed with his "Great Society." Three years later the U.S. found itself in a costly, very unpopular war. The main reason for the inability of America to achieve objectives was because of the strategy adopted for a police action or a limited war.

There was what could be described as continued micromanaging of the war that ended in thousands of casualties both military and civilian, not to mention the destruction of natural resources, infrastructure, and financial costs to everyone; except for those making money from the war.

Arthur Davidson, could not think of much else since he left Jamie at the shuttle area. Chester Blackstone was his Battalion Commander in the Vietnam conflict. He was a hell of a man. He invoked loyalty and strength in the soldiers who followed him.

He was strong and capable, always willing to help those who served under him.

His mind drifted back to one of the worst times they ever spent together as comrades; the battle of Hamburger Hill. Blackstone and the battalion fought their way up a mountain against impossible odds, the worst being the terrain. Blackstone had to be able to track locations of friendly units but also know how his own soldiers would react under the worst of situations. After the tenth day of battle, the toll was mind-boggling.

Thousands were wounded and hundreds dead. There were over a million pounds of bombs, and thousands of pounds of napalm used.

You could not see the enemy because of the terrain. The air was humid and putrid to smell. Sweat began to drip off his face just thinking about the screams of pain, blood, bones protruding, flesh hanging off soldiers being carried on makeshift stretchers and the noise.... "the God damn noise."

There were infantry divisions that could not make it in to help because of the inability of those issuing orders from headquarters, to understand how long it would take to get anywhere in that country. One division assigned to help in the invasion spent two days trapped in a ravine which delayed the concentration of combat power to the Hill.

Chester was everywhere. He did not sleep or eat, he just seemed to always be there, holding young men who were dying, giving orders, and supporting his Battalion; "his men" he called them. How many men did he save because he was always there for each, and every one of them? Then…then when the fighting stopped and the American troops claimed the Hill…orders were issued to vacate it.

Art pulled the semi over into the space provided by the trucking firm he worked for. He numbly locked up his truck and strolled to his vehicle. It would be good to crawl into that bed next to his wife, to smell the kitchen where she was always fixing something; to pet that old dog Bosco. Art slid into the front seat of his car, hung his head as tears rolled down his cheeks. He whispered, "God bless you Chester; forgive me for leaving her there." "She will be alright, she has your blood."

As Art drove to his home feelings of guilt began to overtake him, he muttered, "did I do the right thing?" "Chester, I owe you my life, what should I do?"

CHAPTER XXXV

Victoria was frightened at first when the black-haired stranger grabbed her by the shoulders, but as she swung around to face her she realized she was facing her friend, her sister by name only, Jamie. They embraced immediately with little comment. Victoria was the first to speak in harsh whispered tones, "what are you doing?" "Everyone is looking for you." "What is going on now, I thought you were getting better?"

"Calm down Vicky, I am ok, it's just that I had to get out of there." "I was suffocating, and no one understood what I was going through."

"Well, why can't you take a trip or something like a normal person?" "Half the country is looking for you and you have scared the shit out of everyone…. again." "You had a maniac attack you and nearly kill you, why shouldn't everyone be afraid you are in danger again?" "I am so mad at you, and what have you done to yourself?" "You look like my sixth-grade teacher." Jamie giggled at this statement. "What is funny about this…huh?"

"Look, honey, you are just going to have to trust me on this." "I need to borrow some cash from you."

"You want to borrow money from me?" "Really, are you serious?" "I am not giving you money without an explanation." "No, I mean it; consider this tough love." "No nothing until you tell me why all this, and what for, and then I will think about not calling the police if I believe you."

Jamie had never seen her little friend this angry and defiant before. She was both shocked and impressed. "Alright, I will tell you everything, but let's go to a place more private than this soda shop."

"How did you know where to find me, Jamie?"

"You kidding, you are a creature of habit." "You have stopped by this place to buy a strawberry soda every day after class since I met you."

"Well Jamie because of you, I am not in Europe." "So, you are lucky I am here." "Let's go to Ernie's Coffee around the corner." "We can sit in back and nobody will care."

"I'm right behind you."

They walked silently up the block and around the corner to a little coffee shop they had been in many times. The front of the shop was noted for various varieties of coffee and tea. The glass cupboards were filled with pastries and bagels. In the back of the shop was a dimly lit area with booths and a few bistro tables; a small stage in the corner for aspiring speakers, and musicians for late hours on the weekends. Right now the only people setting there were Jamie, and Victoria.

"Tell me why you are missing Europe because of me."

"I was going there for a semester as an exchange student to study Business and International Law, and you spoiled that," Victoria hissed through clenched teeth. "I got the call on my way to the airport from Audrey." "That poor woman."

"So, you came back because of me?"

"Of course, I did, what is the matter with you?" "After I heard about that note you left, I wanted to choke you." "I gave up, and went back to class because they filled my spot for Europe."

Jamie, sat staring at Victoria, finally responding "I am sorry I did this to you, I really am."

"Just tell me what you are doing here, why you ran away, and why are you dressed like that?" "What happened to your hair?

Jamie began to carefully articulate her plan to Victoria to face Sophia. Victoria, sat with her eyes opening wide exclaiming "you plan to kill her?"

"Shhh…keep your voice down."

"I cannot be a part of this Jamie." "What the fuck are you doing?" "You want to spend the rest of your life in prison?"

"Now Jamie was talking with deep emotion in whispered yet elevated tones, "that woman killed my mother, Charles, caused the death of my grandfather, and ruined any life I had left." "I might as well be in prison because I am dead." "In my heart, I am dead already." Angry tears rolled down her face as she glared at Victoria. This was someone Victoria had not seen before. They sat there gazing into each other's eyes without saying a word.

Victoria finally spoke, "Jamie, listen to me, you do not know for sure Sophia had anything to do with your mother's death or Charles." "Your grandfather died of a heart attack, and you are letting this destroy you." "You nearly got yourself killed." "Please do not do this." "Do not put me in this position." "What about all of us who love you?" "What about Ronnie, and Alex, Audrey, and your father…and me, what about me?" Now Victoria was crying as well. "You cannot kill your grandmother, you cannot."

"Alright…alright, that was harsh and maybe I did not mean to say 'kill her, even though I feel like it." "I want to face her, and tell her how much she hurt me, and all those I love." "I promise you I am just going to talk to her, and then I will leave her alone, and go home." "I ran because I did not need someone trying to talk me out of this." "I was constantly being monitored by this Priest." "Reading Bible passages to me, and Aunt Audrey looking at me all the time with those sad eyes of hers." "My father popping in, and out, always with some excuse that he had to be somewhere else before he hardly got through the door." "And Alex, …. Oh God, Alex."

"What happened with Alex?

"He came to see me, and it was so good to see him." "So easy to talk to him and hold him…." "I just needed him so bad, I needed him to really hold me and kiss me…"

"So, you had sex with him."

"Yes, yes," Jamie, was holding her head and speaking, "it was wonderful sex." "I…. I don't know what happened." "He left angry and upset." "I just feel so bad, and I felt so empty, but I had to do this…. I have to do this."

"Jamie, why can't you see?" "He loves you, I mean really loves you." "You are just using him for sex, and to make yourself feel better, and he is not stupid."

"Wait a minute, I am not using him, I love him." "He is my best friend."

"Your best friend?" "You are calling him your best friend who you know will do anything for you, including fuck you when you get the urge." "Why do you think a wildly attractive man after having sex would get mad, and run away?" "Because he loves you like a man…not a best friend." "You hurt him, you used him….and then you say you felt empty." "Did it ever occur to you that you love him as a man…not just a friend?' "By the way, heard from Ronnie lately?"

"No."

"He has a kid now you know."

"What?" "How do you know that?"

"When you were in the hospital he talked to me a little."

"And?"

"He got involved with that woman you caught him with that night, and she ended up pregnant." "He has a little boy Jamie." "I don't think he has ever seen that child." "He takes care of them with the money, but has nothing to do with her, or I guess the baby." "He was there the whole time you were serious."

Jamie sat in silence.

"Look there is no doubt he has always loved you, but I do not think him abandoning this child is right, and I think he uses his love for you as an excuse." "Alex, never left your side." "He was there for Chester, Audrey, and you." "He is a wonderful person, and you just have always taken him for granted." "When are you planning this meeting with your grandmother?"

"Tomorrow."

"When do you need this money, and how much?"

"Couple thousand."

"Where are you staying?"

"No more questions." "Can I get it now, and then I will call you tomorrow?"

"Yes…but you have to promise me you will not hurt anyone." "Questioning her only, and then you will call?"

"I promise."

"I need to go to the bank to get the money, do you want to wait here for me?"

"Yes, please Vicky, I need some time alone; I feel sick."

"I know," Victoria kissed Jamie on the head; "I will be back soon."

Jamie sat staring at the coffee in front of her. "He has a son…he has a son," she whispered under her breath.

The trip to the bank did not take Victoria long. She placed two thousand dollars in small bills in a paper envelope from the bank. Walking back to the coffee shop she could not shake off the nauseating feeling that seemed to envelop her. "Am I doing the right thing?" She whispered to herself. Could she trust Jamie at this point? What if she really did intend to kill Sophia? She would be an accomplice. Victoria sat down on the park bench just outside the coffee shop. She was breathing hard and in a cold sweat. Her mind was racing, "I cannot enable her, I cannot do this." "Should I call the police?" "Will she ever forgive me?" Finally, Victoria stood up, and headed to the coffee shop with the intention of telling Jamie she must turn herself into the police, and call Audrey; end this insanity. Victoria searched the coffee shop in vain. Jamie was nowhere to be found.

CHAPTER XXXVI

There were at least twelve police and Sheriff patrol cars with sirens on racing toward the Blackstone mansion. Among the officers were detectives Mayes and Andrews. The call had come in from an Arthur Davidson, a truck driver from the Jacksonville, Florida area claiming he had dropped off Jamie Blackstone outside the Jacksonville Airport two days before. The chief of police in Jacksonville was interviewing him that afternoon. Detectives Mayes, and Andrews both felt the safest route, and best chance of finding Jamie was to start at the Blackstone mansion.

"What do you think is going on here?" Detective Mayes stated.

"I just do not know, but my question is of all places for her to run to." "I mean this is where she was running from in the first place when she met up with Mongo." "This makes no sense at all except she is either an extremely smart, and a vicious sociopath or trying to cover up for someone else."

"Why Ann, why would you say sociopath?" "I mean she is guilty of nothing except running away." "She could not have killed Mongo by herself, and if that were even possible, she would have only done everyone a big favor."

"Well even if we could think of things that way, it is not our job to judge the dead guy." "I am sure if she killed him she did it in self-defense." "The question being was she faking the amnesia?" "Does she really believe her grandmother is behind the death of her mother?" "If she does, she would be here for only one reason."

Detective Mayes was getting another call when they pulled up to the mansion. "Remember that little lady, the girl from the hospital when Blackstone was really seriously ill?" "She was Jamie's friend and lives here in Richmond, the classmate."

"Yes, I remember her well." "Why?"

"She just called into the Bureau stating she met with Jamie this afternoon and is afraid she is here to kill her grandmother."

Both detectives were running to the mansion with guns drawn. Officers surrounded the mansion cutting off every exit. Bursting through the front door, and checking every nook, and cranny from the bottom floor to the top floor the only two people found were two elderly cooks; Lydia, who had served the detectives on their last visit to the mansion, and Nora the older of the two. They were sitting at the kitchen counter frightened, and weeping as both detectives placed their guns back in their holsters, and sat beside them. Detective Mayes spoke first, "ladies we are deeply sorry for scaring you like this but can you tell us where Ms. Sophia and Mr. Lewis have gone?"

In a weak voice, Lydia responded, "we don't know that sir." "They don't always tell us when they come and go."

Detective Andrews then questioned, "so how do you know when to have, let's say dinner ready?" "I mean Ms. Blackstone strikes me as the type that would expect everything ready for her, and not have to wait." "Am I correct on that?"

"Sometimes she will tell us to have things ready at a certain time, but now she doesn't leave that often, and we are expected to have things ready at 6:00pm sharp without being asked, so we do that, but she didn't say anything today."

Nora was wiping her eyes as she uttered in a soft voice, "Morrie keeps a calendar in his quarters that he told me about, and he said he writes down anything planned on the calendar."

"Where are his quarters that you are talking about?" Detective Mayes said.

"It is the apartment under the back stairwell." "I can show you if you like?"

"No mam, I want you to stay right where you are." "Thank you for your help." "One other question, have either of you heard from or seen Jamie Blackstone?" Both women looked to be in wide-eyed shock, shaking their heads, "no."

"The detectives entered Morrie's apartment that was orderly, and clean. "Do you see a calendar anywhere?" Detective Andrews called out.

"Yeah, I do, it is hanging right here, and it says.... hair appointment." "No time, address, or nothing." "But here we go, it is in this address book right here that has a salon listed." "It is the only one that I can see listed, and it's on Regency...751 Regency." "Let's go," said detective Mayes "and I will call headquarters on our way."

Before leaving the two detectives stepped back into the kitchen. Detective Andrews spoke gently "you are both free to return to your duties, and again we are sorry we frightened you." "We ask that you tell no one that we were here for right now that is, and if they should return or call, we ask that you call this number on my card immediately, and say nothing to them you are doing so." "Do you understand all this?" Both shook their heads, "yes."

Lydia asked, "are they in trouble?"

"No one is in trouble, we are looking for Jamie Blackstone, and there are some details that surround that situation and we are asking for your full cooperation in this investigation." "There will be a patrol car here, for the time being, parked in front."

CHAPTER XXXVII

Sophia was her usual miserable self at the hairdresser. She was unhappy with the stylist; a new young girl who was a substitute for the woman who normally styled her hair. Debra was also the owner of the salon but had contracted some sort of an illness which took her out of work at her own establishment. Sophia was incensed that she paid these prices to have her hair done and did not get the quality she expected. She was even more incensed when excusing herself to go to the bathroom, there was a sign hanging on the door it was out of order and she would need to go to another bathroom toward the back of the building, muttering to herself, "I am seriously going to look for another salon that will appreciate my business." Just as she was about to open the door, she felt a hard jab to her rib cage. There was an object that was pressing against her thin frame hurting her. It felt like cold steel as she attempted to grab at what was hurting her. For just a fleeting second, she thought she heard something familiar about the fierce hissing voice that instructed her to go through the door to her right or they would kill her. As Sophia stepped through the door to the outside, she faced a car in the alleyway parked extremely close to the building.

"Turn to your right, now." "Walk forward until I tell you to stop." Sophia was shaking so hard she could barely keep herself up. She thought she would be getting into the car, but instead, they walked ahead of where the car was parked. "Stop right here and do not move until I tell you to."

Sophia kept thinking, "I know that voice, who would do this?"

As Sophia stood quivering, she felt someone roughly place a blindfold over her eyes, leaving a small area that she could see out the bottom. She knew someone was sliding a door open. It sounded like a heavy door. "Turn to your right, and do you see the stairway?" "Look down…. now!" "Do you see the stairs?"

"Yes, yes I see them but I can't go down them." "I am shaking and I will fall." "Why are you doing this…why?"

Sophia was starting to unravel, she was crying, and her voice starting to elevate. "Shut-up and start walking down these stairs or I will push you down them and drag you where I want you to go." "Now move slowly…now!" Again, the hard object pushed into Sophia's ribs. She slowly inched down the stairs clinging to the wall. She heard the sliding door again, shuddering as she realized it shut tightly behind her. She was terrified suspecting that she would not come out of this alive. The voice was not saying anything, but she could hear the breathing behind her and hear the footsteps. The stairway was long and narrow. It took her some time to reach the bottom. "Turn to your right again."

"I think I am going to be sick."

"Then bend over and vomit if you need to, but you will keep going until I tell you to stop." Sophia could see old bottles on the floor, and there was a nauseating smell of hops. "Now turn left." They seemed to go into another dark room, and Sophia saw a light come on. At this point, the blindfold ripped from her face, and she was shoved onto a bed. "Sit up and look at me." Sophia was dazed and confused, she could not believe her eyes as she looked up, and there was a Jamie that she barely recognized pointing a gun in her face.

"Jamie Blackstone, what do you think you are doing?" Sophia shrieked.

At this point, Jamie, pushed Sophia down hard on the bed pushing her knee into Sophia's fragile chest and shoving a gun up under her chin. Sophia was frozen with fear seeing the fierceness, and anger in Jamie's face and her eyes seemed to emanate hate.

"Listen to me old woman, you will not ever tell me or anyone else what to do again." "Do you get that.... huh?"

Sophia nodded her head as best she could, to indicate she did understand and would obey Jamie. "Now, we are going to have a little talk." "First we will discuss the rules." "You will keep your voice down because I have very good hearing, and the sound of your hysterics reminds me of an old screeching owl and makes me very nervous." "You do not want me nervous at this point." "No one will find us anyway." "This is an old wine cellar, and brewery left over from the prohibition days, and long forgotten." "Now sit up, and listen carefully." Jamie sat down in a chair directly across from Sophia but stayed positioned close enough to keep Sophia frightened. "Second, I am going to ask you some questions, and I want answers." "I have no regard for you whatsoever so warning; I will shoot you, and leave you to rot down here if I am not given the answers I want." "Do you understand everything I am saying?" Sophia nodded her head. Jamie noticed her pallor which seemed even grayer in color, and for a fleeting second, she thought "I hope she does not die of a heart attack right in front of me".

CHAPTER XXXVIII

The reaction at the Salon of Beauty was much like the reaction at the Blackstone ranch. Shock as well as terror on the faces of the women in the salon when the Richmond PD invaded the salon. "Ladies, we apologize for not giving you a warning that we were coming, but that was totally impossible under the circumstances." "If we frightened you we apologize," said Detective Mayes. One of the officers stepped forward to inform Detective Andrews they had cleared the building, and there was no sign of Jamie or Sophia Blackstone.

Detective Andrews spoke to the clientele in the salon, "who was the operator for Sophia Blackstone in this salon today?"

A small young dark-headed woman meekly stated, "I did her hair today."

"How long ago did she leave?"

"Well, actually she didn't leave." "I mean she wasn't supposed to leave."

"What do you mean by that?" "She wasn't supposed to leave?"

"I mean she just excused herself to go to the bathroom, and she never came back." "I hadn't completed styling her hair."

With that statement, Detective Andrews turned to the police officer in charge and instructed them to make another sweep of the building.

Detective Mayes clearly exasperated, "this is getting embarrassing, I mean this disappearing act that Blackstone is able to pull off, now even with her grandmother possibly as a prisoner, and we let this happen again?"

"Calm down," Detective Andrews stated sternly, "we do not know that for sure." "We need to make sure there is not a place somewhere in these old buildings that she may be holding her."

After a minute or so of silence, Detective Mayes responded, "I am going to go look around myself in this building." "This just does not make sense."

"Go ahead, I am going to talk with these ladies a bit more." "If you hear anything, or see anything please call me right away."

"Yeah, you do the same."

Detective Mayes walked around the building, the block, and from the top of the building to the bottom. He had carefully climbed the stairs to the attic looking in every corner, and crevice for some clue on where Jamie could have taken her grandmother. He found an old staircase leading to the basement in the front of the building. Descending down into the dank darkness gave him the shivers. The nauseating smell reminded him of the smell of cheap marijuana, and rotting potatoes, pervading the basement area, and seemed to get worse as he continued down the narrow stairway. He nearly urinated down his leg when two officers stepped out of a side room just off the bottom step. "Fuck!" "I nearly pissed my pants here."

"Sorry, sir," one of the policemen sheepishly responded. "We found this part of the building, and thought we better check it out."

"You find anything?"

"Nah, it's empty." "Few old rooms, some old furniture, and that is about it."

"What is that smell?" "Smells like someone has been smoking bad pot down here."

"It's hops, sir."

"Hops?"

"Yeah, my pop used to brew beer in a shed outside our home." "Smelled just like this from the hops he added." "It does smell kinda like old pot, or worse."

"Makes me want to puke." "Does not smell like any good beer I have ever had." "Let's get out of here." "One question though, wouldn't someone have to be down here brewing for it to smell like this?" "I mean there isn't anything down here, so why?"

"Some of these old buildings had breweries in the basements." "They kept them hid in these places before we were ever born." "That smell just does not go away." "Kind of like a porta potty always smells like shit."

CHAPTER XXXIX

Jamie had left the basement where she had Sophia. The smell of the area was making her sick, and she knew she needed to get some pain, and nausea medication for Sophia. She was going to get answers if it killed them both. The police were everywhere around the building as she knew they would be. She made her way across the alley, and in through a back entrance to the cigar and smoke shop on the next block. She knew the hallway running down a corridor, and out the front door. Not far down the block was a drug store. Again, she had a disguise making her look close to homeless if you did not look too closely. They had protein drinks and snacks. She was going to keep Sophia alive until she gave her the answers, "then I do not care." "I swear to God, I do not care," she muttered under her breath. She managed to avoid the police, and make her way down the stairway. As she went down the steps she marveled at how easy it had been to accomplish all she had right under the nose of the authorities, not once, but now several times. "I should have been a jewel thief." "Not for the riches, but for the excitement," she thought. Again, thinking out loud, "instead I watch one person after another I love, die for no good reason." Thinking about this made her angry, and helped her focus.

As she rounded the corner, and entered the room she stopped and held her breath. "Was she dead?" Sophia was lying very still on her back with her eyes open. Her lips were purple, her breathing so shallow she could barely detect it, and there was a smell of old sweat. She grabbed Sophia's clothing and jerked her up. Her skin was clammy but she did respond. "Take these pills, and drink this, all of it."

"Wh...what is it?"

"Enteric coated aspirin, and a protein drink." "Now do it." Sophia did not argue. It took her a long time to drink the protein as Jamie sat quietly across from her, staring at Sophia with hatred in her eyes, and contemplating her next move. She decided that she would give her 30 minutes for the aspirin to help with any pain or heart issues, and the drink to stabilize her blood sugar. Both health issues she knew Sophia struggled with, in a normal situation.

"Can I have more water?" Sophia meekly asked.

Jamie stood pouring her more water into a paper cup, and not saying a word but continuing the glare.

"Can you tell me what I have done to deserve this?" "Why do you hate me so?"

With that, Jamie leaned close "you must be kidding." "As I said in the beginning, you shut the hell up, and speak only when you are answering the questions I ask, nothing more or you will never see the outside of this crap hole again." "Got that?"

Sophia shook her head "yes" keeping her eyes cast downward.

CHAPTER XL

The phone was ringing, and a voice almost too quiet to hear answered, "Hello, this is Victoria."

"Victoria, this is Victor Blackstone." "There are several of us here on this call." "Aunt Audrey called everyone together, so it is Alex, Ron, myself, and of course Audrey." Detective Miranda was also present, and recording the call. "Audrey received a call from the authorities about the conversation they had with you earlier today, and what you told them about Jamie." "We are all here, and very worried to say the least." "Can you tell us what is going on as far as you know; is Jamie safe right now?" "Do you know?"

"I do not know where she is, or if she is safe." Victoria was crying and trying her best to answer between sobs.

"Take some deep breaths honey, and try to relax." "Just do your best to tell us what happened when Jamie approached you," Victor said in a calm soft voice.

After a long pause, Victoria responded; "I was on my way home from class, and she came up behind me." "She does not look the same." "Her hair is short and black." "She said she needed some cash, and was going to talk to Sophia." Another long pause; "at one point she said she wanted to kill her." There was an audible breath from Audrey. Victor felt cold chills running over him as Victoria continued. "She seemed sad and somewhat hopeless about her life; like.... umm...like it was over, and she had nothing to lose." There was a long pause on the call, no one said a word as each person tried to cope with what was being said. "Jamie feels like Sophia is responsible for the deaths of her mother, Charles, as well as her grandfather." Again silence, "she talked about all of you." "She promised me she would not hurt Sophia if I gave her some cash." "That she would just talk to Sophia, and ask her questions, and then she would call me." "I believed her like the fool I am." Victoria stopped for a period of time while trying to compose herself, and take a sip of the tea that her mother had made for her. It warmed her inside but did not help to control the shaking of her hands nor the sadness that encircled her. "I went to the bank, and made up my mind when I was coming back that I was not going to let her go, and I was not going to give her the money." "I decided I was going to talk her into going to the authorities that she had not done anything wrong and we could work it out." "But when I returned, she was gone...." "I checked everywhere ..but," her voice faded. With that Victoria began to cry uncontrollably. Her mother took the phone and stated Victoria could not talk anymore.

"Sarah, I know this is very hard on Victoria, but I cannot tell you how important this is to try to figure out where Jamie is right now" Victor pleaded. "I need to ask Victoria some questions, so I am willing to wait until she can talk to me again." Sarah, Victoria's mother was quiet, but Victor could hear her talking to Victoria.

"Victor,"

"Yes,"

"This is Victoria again," she said very softly. "I am sorry, but..."

"Listen, honey," Victor cut her off, "I just have a couple more questions, and then I promise to leave you alone, but I will keep you informed of anything we find out." "Ok?" "You said she talked about all of us, can you tell me specifically what was said?"

"She said you called once in a while and made excuses about places you needed to go." A pang of guilt came over Victor. "She said Audrey was always staring at her with sad eyes, and the priest was driving her crazy with his visits." "She talked about Ron, and did not know he had a child." "She seemed troubled by that, and wanted to be left to think; that is when I went to the bank." Victoria inwardly hoped it was hurting Ronnie as she talked about his child, and how it affected Jamie. "She talked about Alex, and how she loved him." "She felt guilty about some meeting or interaction they had and was sorry it did not end well." Both Ronnie, and Alex stood immobile, and silent as Victor glared at them. "I do not know what else to say." "She would not tell me where she was staying, just that she would call me."

"I understand, and I will let you go now." Exchanging glances with Detective Miranda who nodded to confirm the end of the call. "I am sorry this has been hard on you Victoria." "I want you to know we appreciate you contacting the authorities, talking with us, and we will let you know of anything that is going on." "However, it is important that you also let everyone know if you hear from Jamie."

"Oh yes, I know there is a police car parked outside the house and makes regular rounds."

"Alright then honey, take care of yourself."

"Bye Victor," Victoria said in a mouthed response.

CHAPTER XLI

"Why did you have my mother killed?" Jamie sat close to Sophia even though it repulsed her in every way she wanted to be as intimidating as possible. She really wanted to pull the gun from her purse, put it to Sophia's head, and pull the trigger. Sophia did not answer her but kept gazing down toward the floor. At that point, Jamie did pull out the gun and held it close to Sophia's forehead.

Sophia winced jerking backward, "No, no please no," now shaking her head back, and forth rapidly, which nearly knocked the gun from Jamie's hand. "I didn't try to have her killed."

Jamie's frustration was wearing thin, and she could feel it turning to utter fury against this woman. She wanted to end her life like Sophia had ended her mother's. "You are a liar!" Jamie yelled into Sophia's ear. "A liar!" "There was a man in prison who admitted he was hired for a hit in Gray Mountain, and Mongo, your little friend also said he was hired."

337

"Mongo was not my friend," Sophia yelled back as loud as she could in a hoarse scratchy voice. "No one was hired to kill her, just scare her!"

Jamie leaned back from Sophia's face again putting the gun to Sophia's temple, and speaking through gritted teeth, "I am tired of this game, and the smell of you." "You will start from the beginning, and slowly explain to me what happened." "If you don't I am going to get that dilapidated old smelly pillow next to you, and fire a bullet through it into your brain." "Now, right now talk!" Sophia was shaking so hard she could barely sit upright. She opened her mouth to speak, and nothing came out but a squeak. Jamie held a cup with water to her mouth, "drink this, and then I mean it start talking or I am done." Sophia had difficulty swallowing the water and began to cough violently. The more she coughed the worse the cough became for her to control. "Drink this one sip at a time until you stop that." Sophia did as she was told but each time she tried to speak the coughing would start again. Jamie grabbed her blouse, and with that Sophia passed completely out. For a short time, Jamie thought she might be dead but Sophia had a pulse, and was breathing normally. Jamie sat in the chair opposite the bed, and drank a soda watching Sophia closely, and thinking to herself "we are not leaving until I get some answers." She was fully prepared to accept Sophia's death, and her incarceration if that is what it took.

Sophia began to wake up after a few minutes. As soon as she opened her eyes she began to sob "no, no I can't do this, please just let me go, please, please let me go, I won't tell anyone."

Jamie flew at Sophia grabbing her around her neck and squeezing as hard as she could. Sophia kept shaking her head back and forth attempting to scratch Jamie's hands away from her neck. Her color was deteriorating into a grayish purple, and saliva spewed from her mouth covering Jamie's hands. Her hands began to slip reducing her grip, and the smell of Sophia's breath was making her gag. Jamie let go of Sophia and began wiping her hands on sanitation towels she had in her bag waiting for Sophia to recover.

"I was worried about my son," Sophia said in between coughs. Jamie, froze in place listening to every utterance. "Mongo was a friend of a friend that had done some work for him." "I just asked him to scare her enough that she would not ever try to contact Victor again." "He was talking about going back to her." "He would not stop drinking, and I was afraid he would leave again for good." Sophia stopped for a moment and asked for water. Jamie had not moved an inch since Sophia started talking. She handed her a paper cup with more water in it and sat quietly. "Mongo hired someone, and I do not know who." "As far as I know he never actually laid eyes on Mary." "He just had a picture." "When I learned of Mary's death, I contacted Mongo; he said the men were drunk and got in a fight." "They were fighting over the gun, and it fired." "Don't you see, she was never supposed to die, it was an accident?"

CHAPTER XLII

Victor stood staring down at the phone. He could not get the statement that Jamie had made out of his mind, "I made up excuses to be somewhere." Did he sound that way? Did he actually sound like he was avoiding his daughter after all these years of being neglectful? Could Jamie have been driven to mental illness? Driven far enough to kill her grandmother? He distrusted and personally disliked his own mother. She had driven him to drink and caused estrangement from his father, daughter, and dear Mary who he truly loved but was not strong enough to defend; such cowardice. But he could never harm Sophia. Had he caused this? "Oh God," shaking his head as he covered his face.

The harsh voices made Victor look up, "so just exactly what did you say or do to Jamie to make her run again?" Ronnie had walked closer to Alex with an angry scowl on his face. "What did you do to her?"

Alex whirled around facing Ronnie head on, "you bastard, you lying, cheating bastard." "How dare you say a word to me when you led her on, and then cheated on her, and now you are deserting your own flesh and blood." They were now within inches from each other, red-faced and fists clenched.

"You haven't answered my question, what did you do?" Ronnie said yelling at Alex.

Just as they were about to wrestle to the ground Victor stepped between them pushing Ronnie backward into the end table and Alex pushed forward toward Ronnie. Victor was now yelling at both of them, "Stop it, damn it stop!"

Now they all stopped when they heard a woman screaming. Audrey was yelling, "get out of my house!" "Get out!" "This is my home, and you will not show me or my late husband this kind of disrespect!"

Detective Miranda stepped in front of Audrey, "you heard the lady, get out."

Alex was the first to respond, "I am so sorry for my behavior, please forgive me." "You know I have always adored you, and Ralph, please forgive," as he bowed his head, and moved forward to embrace her.

Detective Miranda pushed Alex back before he could touch her. "It is ok Detective Miranda, I know Alex well and I know he means it."

Victor also apologized, and Ronnie simply nodded his head in an effort to admit his guilt. "Audrey said in a soft voice, "please let's all sit down and have some coffee, and act like civilized adults." "We are not helping anyone with this kind of hateful thinking."

All of the men sat at the kitchen table as Detective Miranda spoke to Audrey. "Mrs. Keck, I have a plane to catch to Richmond." "I appreciate the offer but if you think you will be alright with this bunch, then I must go."

"Of course, I will be fine, and I appreciate you intervening on my behalf."

"You are welcome, and if we hear anything we will notify you immediately, but please you do the same for us."

"Of course, we all will call if we have any contact with Jamie."

With that Detective Miranda left the house, and Audrey served coffee to quiet remorseful men.

After a period of quiet Victor finally spoke. "I would like your honest opinion; do you think Jamie felt like I was avoiding her?"

Alex responded quickly, "how honest do you want me to be here?"

"Completely honest."

"I think Jamie has always felt like you have been avoiding her, and quite frankly sir, you have." "The only time you ever paid any attention to her was when she lay dying in a hospital bed."

Even though Victor was surprised, and a little embarrassed by Alex's harsh words, he was not offended. "Well Alex, I accept what you are saying." "I think the avoidance is simply nothing more than shame." "Jamie is a beautiful lady, and at times reminds me so much of Mary." "I felt guilty every time I looked at her." "Between the shame, and the feeling of hopelessness when Sophia started her nagging; the bottle was the only place left for me, at least that is what I thought." "I just did not think Jamie believed that was going on right now." "I have not been avoiding her lately; I just have been busy with the business my father left."

Audrey walked to Victor's side and placed her hand on his shoulder. "I think Jamie's perception of life right now is just skewed." "She seemed to improve drastically over the last few weeks." "I think she was making a decision at that time." "A decision, and a plan to find out the truth about what happened to her mother." "What you do not know is, the authorities found the supplies she left behind."

"What supplies?" Ronnie asked.

"Supplies like a flotation device to carry clothes and things." "She also left a wet-suit." "She must have had her clothing in some kind of waterproof bag because old Sam the bus driver said everything looked normal when she boarded the bus." "Jamie planned this, and I think she planned it weeks ago; very carefully." "The man who gave her a ride to the east coast was a trucker, and I have not heard all the details yet, but he was apparently chosen randomly."

"I knew something was not right." Alex now had everyone's attention. He gazed off away from the others. "Even though she seemed to be improving from her previous moods, she just seemed distant in another world." "I felt like it was all an act at one point." "I confronted her about it, and she had an answer for everything." "Her responses seemed to be a diversion from the truth." Alex was silent for a period of time. "As a matter of fact, we had a disagreement about it." "I was bloody sick of it." "She was always treating me like a brother and confidant one minute, and a boy toy the next."

"Brother, confidant is fine, perfect, but I have loved Jamie for a long time; not just as a brotherly friend." "I wanted her to know that, and I was frustrated, so I just left." "I was angry so I did not try to contact her after that." Alex's voice faded and the room remained silent until the members one by one made the excuse to leave, and keep in touch if any news was heard.

CHAPTER XLIII

"What you are telling me is my mother died because of an accident? "Her life was taken from her, and her family because you wanted to scare her?" "Is that right so far Sophia?" "Just how were these drunken men supposed to scare my mother?" "Answer me!"

Sophia was exhausted and terrified. How was she ever going to see the light of day again? She had no choice but to continue this interrogation hoping and praying someone would find them before she died in this awful place. "Ricky arranged this, so I did not have the details, I just paid him."

"His name is Mongo." "You must have been friendly to call him Ricky." "Who was the friend who introduced you to...Ricky Mongo?" Sophia did not answer right away, so Jamie charged toward her.

"It was Ted Ames," Sophia quickly and urgently answered. "His name was Ted Ames!" "He was my banker, and knew Mongo."

"One more time, how were they going to scare her?"

"They were going to wait until closing, and kidnap her." "They were going to act like Victor had sent them, and warn her to never contact him again." "I need to urinate."

"There is a room right outside this room to the left, use it." "I will be right here, try to run and I will catch you before you take three steps."

"I do not know if I can walk over there."

"Well grandmother, you are going to have a hell of a time climbing the steps to get out of here, aren't you?"

Sophia edged herself to the end of the bed. She followed the wall slowly to the doorway. Right after going through the door Jamie heard her gasp. "There is no toilet here, no paper," she began to weep. Jamie stepped through the door and handed Sophia a sanitary wipe. "But...but I am wet."

"That is hardly my problem, is it?" Jamie turned, and walked back into the room she was keeping Sophia in, and waited. Sophia finally came back through the door."

"Can I have another wipe at least?"

"Keep it civil Sophia, show me some respect at all times or I will just leave you here chained to this bed." Jamie handed Sophia another wipe, and Sophia sat down on the end of the bed.

"Tell me about Charles."

"Why do you want to know about him?" "Why is he your concern?" Jamie reached in her bag and pulled out a small chain, and padlock. As she started stepping forward Sophia put her hands up, "Alright, alright." "He disgusted me, always rambling around; I could not stand him, and you a Blackstone, riding around the ranch with him on that cart." "I was so embarrassed, and it showed disrespect for the family."

"He was my dear friend!" Jamie screamed at Sophia. "Everyone loved him, everyone, including my father, and grandfather who you also drove to his grave." "Charles hurt no one, and you had him murdered."

"No, I did not," Sophia responded in as loud a voice as she could. "When I met with Mongo I told him about Charles, but I swear to you I did not have him murdered." "Mongo just took it upon himself to kill him." "I did not pay him anything." "I did not want Charles dead, there was no reason for that." "Your grandfather had a heart attack which you caused!" Sophia retracted in horror when she realized what she had just said. She ducked down slightly knowing what might be coming next.

Jamie sat still watching Sophia thinking over everything carefully. Sophia did not move as Jamie reached into her bag again. Instead of bringing out the gun or chains that Sophia expected, she brought out a tablet and began writing. An hour passed as Jamie continued to write on the tablet. Sophia had lain back on the bed, and was now sleeping.

When Sophia opened her eyes and realized she was still in the dark humid filthy place she closed her eyes and she wept. Her head was pounding, and the nausea was overwhelming. She raised herself to a sitting position and saw the note at the end of the bed, which said, "you are free to go."

She called out, "is anyone out there?" Sophia expressed a sigh of relief when there was silence. Then she said out loud, "oh God, please help me get out of here." The hall was dark with very dim lighting at the very end. She moved slowly clutching the walls as she made her way toward the stairway she was forced down. The smell was so thick and pungent, she stopped to gag and retch several times along the way. She reached the steps and knew she would need to crawl to the top, using both her hands and feet to make it. She stopped to rest on the steps reserving as much energy as she could in order to open the large heavy door at the top of the stairs, praying it was not locked. Sophia had nearly reached the top when the door slid open with a loud bang! There stood a detective and several police officers.

"Thank God you are here."

CHAPTER XLIV

It was very late that evening when Audrey heard someone knocking at the front door. She was hesitant to answer until she saw the police cruiser in the driveway, and Victor looking through the glass. "Victor, what is it, what is wrong?" "Was Jamie found?"

Victor had a somewhat empty look on his face. "I do not know how to explain this, so I will let you read it." "This letter was delivered to the hotel marked as urgent addressed to me about 20 minutes ago." "I called the police right away." "That is why they are here." "They brought me here, and are on the phone with Richmond PD right now."

Audrey sat down on a kitchen chair, and began to read the letter:

Dear Aunt Audrey, and Father, please forgive me for all that I have done. I have found what I have been looking for; the truth. I realize I have a great deal to account for, and certainly, I will atone for my sins, and ask God's forgiveness, but I have peace now. The police can fill you in on the details.

I have written a complete accounting of what happened before I was attacked, and the events that followed. Sophia is with the police in Richmond; she is safe and unharmed. I have one more thing I must do before I surrender to the police. I love you both with all my heart. Please notify Victoria, and anyone else you feel should be given this information. I will contact Alex myself. I will be in touch with you soon. Love, Jamie

Alex had been out walking on the beach. He was an insomniac anyway, but tonight sleep was impossible. He could hear his phone and raced up the stairs to answer it. There was silence, "dammit who called me?"

"Do you still fly?"

"Who is this?"

"Me baby, Jamie." "I was just hoping you could come and get me?"

"Where are you?"

"Richmond."

"What is going on, are you safe?" Alex could not believe what was happening, his heart was pounding and he was breaking out in a sweat. "The police are looking everywhere for you."

Jamie chuckled, "Yes I know." "It won't be long my darling, and if you will have me, I want to be with you the rest of my life." "I love you with all my heart, and after I finish paying for all I have done, I never want to leave your side again."

Tears welled up in Alex's eyes, as he stood listening; speechless.

"Are you there Alex?"

"Yes, I am here."

"I have so much to tell you before I turn myself into the police."

CHAPTER XLV

Detective Mayes was angry and disgusted when his phone woke him up from a great dream about the waitress at the bistro he had been visiting daily.

"Hey, are you awake?" Detective Andrews said questioning in a firm voice.

"Well fuck no I was not awake." "What time is it anyway?"

"I don't know about 3:00am but get your ass up, and get down here." "We have Sophia Blackstone."

Detective Mayes hung up the phone without saying another word. Detective Christianson had received the call where to find Sophia Blackstone, along with directions on where to find the recordings of her confessions

THE END